The Stupendously Spectacular Spelling Bee

The Stupendously SPECTACULAR Spelling Bee

DEBORAH ABELA

Cover design by Aleksei Bitskoff
Cover and internal illustrations by Aleksei Bitskoff

Published by Sourcebooks Jabberwocky, an imprint of Sourcebooks, Inc.
P.O. Box 4410, Naperville, Illinois 60567-4410
(630) 961-3900
Fax: (630) 961-2168
sourcebooks.com

Originally published in 2016 in Australia by Penguin Random House Australia Pty Ltd, an imprint of Penguin Random House.

Library of Congress Cataloging-in-Publication Data

Names: Abela, Deborah, 1966- author.
Title: The Stupendously Spectacular Spelling Bee / Deborah Abela.
Description: Naperville, Illinois : Sourcebooks Jabberwocky, [2018] | "Originally published in 2016 in Australia by Penguin Random House Australia Pty Ltd, an imprint of Penguin Random House." | Summary: Terribly shy, India Wimple is brilliant at spelling and her loving family will do whatever it takes to help her compete in a televised national spelling bee in Sydney, Australia.
Identifiers: LCCN 2017030951 | (13 : alk. paper)
Subjects: | CYAC: Spelling bees--Fiction. | Family life--Australia--Fiction. | Self-confidence--Fiction. | Friendship--Fiction. | Australia--Fiction.
Classification: LCC PZ7.A15937 Stu 2018 | DDC [Fic]--dc23 LC record available at https://lccn.loc.gov/2017030951

Source of Production: Berryville Graphics, Berryville, Virginia, USA
Date of Production: February 2018
Run Number: 5011531

Printed and bound in the United States of America.
BVG 10 9 8 7 6 5 4 3 2 1

TH

Thank you, Jazzy and Declan, for sharing
what it's like to be champion spellers.

To Catherine Sumsky, respiratory clinical nurse from the
Sydney Children's Hospital, for her expert asthma advice.

And to Miss Gray, my fourth grade teacher, who
made spelling a stupendously spectacular game.

1

TREMULOUS

(adjective):

Nervous, timid, a little frightened.

The girl felt very tremulous about the challenging task ahead.

INDIA WIMPLE COULD SPELL. BRILLIANTLY. On Friday nights, she and her family would huddle in front of the TV in their pajamas, in their small house in Yungabilla, and watch the Stupendously Spectacular Spelling Bee.

India adored her family—it was the thing that mattered most to her. There was her younger brother, Boo; Mom; Dad; and Nanna Flo.

Nanna Flo hadn't always lived with them. She'd moved in after she fell and broke her wrist during an especially enthusiastic yoga move. She wasn't happy about leaving the home where she'd lived with Grandpop for over forty years. She made kind of a fuss, mostly by stomping around and saying "Fiddlesticks!" a lot, which was as close to swearing as Nanna Flo ever got. But she soon realized she was much happier surrounded by her family, and the stomping and almost swearing stopped.

One particular Friday night, where our story begins, the Wimples huddled in front of the TV, as they usually did. But this night was different. It was the Stupendously Spectacular Spelling Bee Grand Final and, as it happened, it was also the day the Wimples' lives would change forever.

Boo stretched out on the floor with his chin cupped in his hands, while Mom, Dad, Nanna Flo, and India sat snugly on the sofa. Ernie rested at their feet.

Mom, Dad, and Nanna Flo were people. Ernie was a large statue of a bulldog that Nanna Flo insisted on taking with her everywhere, much to her family's embarrassment. Not only was Ernie remarkably heavy, but he was also incredibly ugly and had the unfortunate habit of scaring young children.

On the TV was a tiny, barely there girl with bouncy, black curls, whose mouth was wide open, as if she'd just had a very big shock. Her name was Katerina. After months of spelling bee heats held all around the country, there were only two spellers left. Katerina was one of them, and her mouth was wide open because her opponent had misspelled his last word. He moved aside with a shake of his head and Katerina stepped up to the microphone.

She looked so small standing on the main stage of the Concert Hall at Sydney Opera House. Dwarfed by its huge, arched ceilings, she took a deep breath, looking more like a girl about to fall off a mountain—a very high mountain—than someone who was simply going to spell.

Her body quivered. Her curls shook. It was indeed a *tremulous* moment.

The camera cut to her parents sitting in the front row. Her dad gave her a thumbs-up and her mother raised crossed fingers.

This seemed to make Katerina relax. A little.

But then she looked like she was on top of that mountain again.

Not far from her, sparkling in the stage lights, was the Stupendously Spectacular Spelling Bee trophy. If she spelled the next word correctly, she would be the new champion and the trophy would be hers.

The Concert Hall fell deathly silent as the pronouncer, Philomena Spright, prepared to reveal the next word. Philomena had been the official pronouncer longer than India had been alive. Philomena's hair sat perched on her head in a perfect soft-serve-ice-cream swirl. She always wore very glamorous dresses and heels so high that India worried she might trip over them one day.

But she never did.

Philomena Spright held a small card with her bright-red fingernails in front of her equally bright-red lips.

On the card was written, quite possibly, the final word of the competition.

Very carefully, Philomena pronounced, "*Tremulous,* an adjective meaning nervous, timid, or a little frightened. Using it in a sentence, I could say, *The girl felt tremulous at facing the next word of the spelling bee grand final.*"

The audience quietly chuckled before settling into an anxious silence.

Katerina took a few seconds to think.

In the Wimple family home, far, far away, India whispered the spelling of the word without hesitation.

"That's the right answer, isn't it?" Boo asked.

India's auburn ponytail swung as she nodded. "I'm sure of it."

Katerina crossed both fingers behind her back and began to spell. "Tremulous. T-r-e-m-u-l-o-u-s." She finished by saying the word with one final, hopeful flourish. "Tremulous?"

Philomena Spright paused for effect, which she always did. It was her way of building suspense, of making the audience and the contestants lean in, eager to hear her verdict. She never revealed the result too early by showing a smile or a frown. She stared at the girl for several excruciatingly long seconds before saying, in her most serious voice, "Katerina, I'm afraid that answer is...*correct*!"

It was only then that Philomena Spright smiled a broad, victorious smile. "You are the new Stupendously Spectacular Spelling Bee champion!"

Katerina's hands flew to her cheeks. The lights flashed, theme music blared, and a shower of confetti sprinkled down from above like a colorful snowfall. The audience was on its feet, cheering and clapping.

"You were right," Boo whispered to his sister. "As always."

Philomena Spright handed Katerina the trophy, which was almost too big for her to hold. Her parents rushed onto the stage, crying and hugging their daughter.

When the applause eventually died down, Philomena Spright spoke into the microphone. "Katerina, tell everyone at home how this moment feels."

Katerina hugged the trophy with both hands and thought for a few seconds before saying, "From the time I was a little girl, I've dreamed of winning the Stupendously Spectacular Spelling Bee." She paused, a small tear forming in the corner of her eye. "And now it's really happening."

More tears flowed as Katerina's mom and dad hugged her tight.

"It most certainly is happening," Philomena Spright declared. "From thousands of spellers, competing in hundreds of rounds and one riveting grand final, you are our new champion! And now for your prizes." She took an envelope from the trophy stand. "As always, there is a five-hundred-dollar gift card for Mr. Trinket's Book Emporium."

Katerina accepted it with an awestruck "thank you."

"And that's not all. We can now reveal your grand prize."

There was a drum roll.

The Wimple family listened with great anticipation. There was a different grand prize each time. There'd been a family cruise and a trip to the world's tallest toy store in New York. Once it was a vacation to the Wizarding World of Harry Potter.

"You know how you like amusement parks?" Philomena Spright asked.

"Yes." Katerina nodded feverishly.

"You and your family are going to...Disneyland, with five thousand dollars in spending money!"

Katerina squealed. She couldn't help it—it just came out. "Thank you! Thank you! Thank you!"

"You are welcome, welcome, welcome!"

The family fell into hugs and even more joyful tears.

Philomena Spright turned to the camera. "That's it for another Stupendously Spectacular Spelling Bee. I'd like to thank all our *sensational* spellers and our *astounding* audience. Were you able to spell all the words correctly? Would *you* like the chance to stand on this very stage? If you think you have what it takes, why not sign up?"

She looked down the barrel of the camera and, for a moment, India Wimple thought the pronouncer was speaking only to her. "Because our next Stupendously Spectacular Spelling Bee champion could be *you*!"

Philomena Spright didn't move for what felt like several minutes, pointing her shiny, red fingernail at India with the smallest of knowing smiles on her lips.

2

DISCONCERTING

(adjective):

Unnerving, discomfiting, and more than a little bewildering.

The memory alone was really very disconcerting.

BOO NUDGED HIS SISTER. "PHILOMENA'S right—it could be you."

India scoffed. "Me?"

"Yes," Mom said. "Why not?"

"Because TV is only for the very rich, the very famous, or the very pretty...and I'm not any of those things."

"I disagree!" Dad argued. "It's true we're not rich or famous, but as for being pretty, you are beautiful from your head down to your toes."

"Thanks, Dad, but I think you might be biased."

"Fiddlesticks!" Nanna Flo blurted. "What a load of codswallop! Your father's right or you can dunk me in a barrel of barbecue sauce!"

"It would be exciting to see you onstage with all those other children," Mom said, "showing the world how clever you are."

"It's true." Boo sprang upright in his pajamas, which were a little baggy and covered with planets and stars. "You're the smartest person I know."

"Do you really think I could?" India asked, sounding a bit tremulous herself.

"We *know* you could!" Dad scooted so far forward on the couch that he almost fell off. "Who do I ask when I don't know how to spell a word?"

"India," Boo answered.

"And who sits there spelling every word correctly every single time?"

"India," Boo repeated.

The TV screen was jammed with people laughing and calling Katerina's name, while photographers elbowed their way closer to take her picture. She was totally surrounded. India felt breathless and light-headed.

She sighed. "And who freezes every time she stands in front of an audience?"

There was a pause. Everyone knew who she meant, but they pretended they didn't.

It was true. India Wimple was terribly, horribly shy, and whenever she found herself the center of attention, her cleverness seemed to disappear.

It all started a long time ago, when she had the starring role in her school play, *Matilda*. India loved Roald Dahl's story of the shy but brilliant girl and had been rehearsing for weeks. At home, Boo had helped her practice every day, so she wouldn't forget a word. On opening night, the school halls buzzed, while backstage, the actors nervously muttered lines.

But not India. She knew her role and was ready.

When the play began, India felt as if she were floating. The audience was enthralled and sat glued to every word.

It was all going perfectly—until what happened next.

India saw someone moving in the darkness at the back of the hall. The figure scooped something into his arms and was staggering along the row toward the exit. Another person quickly followed behind. People stood to allow them past. Whispers rippled through the air.

And then she heard a faint series of coughs. India realized the shadowy figure was Dad—he was carrying Boo in his arms. And the person following was Mom. They reached the end of the row and hurried out of the hall.

India shivered and stared after them.

It was only when one of the actors nudged her that India realized the entire cast was waiting for her to speak, but she didn't know what to say. It was as if every line she'd rehearsed had vanished from her memory.

The audience shifted awkwardly in their seats. Some pointed. Others laughed behind their hands.

India froze. She stared at the glowing green exit sign. All she could think of was Boo cradled in Dad's arms, coughing and struggling to breathe.

Boo's asthma could sneak up on an otherwise perfectly fine day and squeeze his lungs so tightly that sometimes he'd even have to be rushed to the hospital and hooked up to special machines to help him breathe.

The play went on, but India missed every cue and messed up every line. The other actors even began saying them for her until finally, somehow, they made it to the end of the show.

Since that day, India had this small, snarky voice inside her head—one that actually got quite loud sometimes—reminding her that she had failed and *would* fail if she ever tried anything like that again.

"Don't you think, India?"

Dad had obviously been talking, but India hadn't heard a thing.

He got to his feet and tightened the belt on his bathrobe. "Because I'm sure of it. So sure, in fact, that I predict that we here tonight, in this humble home in Yungabilla, are in the presence of the next Stupendously Spectacular Spelling Bee champion."

Nanna Flo, Mom, and Boo burst into applause.

India shook the *disconcerting* memory of the play from her mind. "Nice try, everyone, but I don't think it's for me."

"Why not?" Boo's eyes widened beneath his floppy hair. "You'd be amazing!"

"You'd wipe the floor with those other kids!" Nanna Flo sometimes said things that were a little inappropriate, especially if she was worked up.

"Now, now." Dad held up a silencing hand. "It's India's choice. If she'd rather not enter, then as a family we need to respect that."

He paused, only barely able to disguise his real hope. "But if she *were* to try out, she knows she'd have her family behind her one hundred and fifty percent."

He waited for India to be convinced by his heartfelt speech and imploring look.

"There's no such thing as one hundred and fifty percent, Dad, but thanks for understanding."

There was a brief silence, filled with the Wimple family's collective disappointment. But Dad was right—who were they to ask her to do something she didn't want to do, something that would terrify her? She'd made her decision, and they needed to accept that—even if they didn't want to, which sometimes happens in families, as I'm sure you'll know if you live in one.

Dad tried to lift the mood. "Right then, my young Wimples, teeth brushing and story time before bed. Off you go!"

India got to her feet but snuck a quick peek before she left the room. Dad had sunk back onto the sofa, the collar of his bathrobe bunched up around his neck as if he were in danger of disappearing inside.

3

VALOROUS

(adjective):

Brave, fearless, maybe even a little daring.

She made a valorous decision to face her fears.

INDIA COULDN'T SLEEP.

Normally after the excitement of a Stupendously Spectacular Spelling Bee episode, she would nestle into bed, Dad would read a story to her and Boo, and she'd quickly drift off into a dream-filled slumber.

But this night was different.

She couldn't stop her mind from thinking, and the harder she tried to sleep, the more awake she felt. She kept seeing Philomena Spright pointing her shiny, red fingernail at her, telling her she could win.

But could she really?

It was true she spelled every word correctly as she followed along from home. And even when she'd never heard the word before, she had an uncanny ability to work it out.

But it was also true that she was the girl who froze onstage during her school play, unable to remember a single line. What if it happened again? In front of millions?

This was one of those times when the voice inside her head got a little louder: *A girl from Yungabilla could never be the next spelling bee champion. Most people don't even know where Yungabilla is. It isn't a vacation destination. No one famous ever came from here. There are no natural wonders. There aren't even any unnatural wonders, like a giant pineapple or shrimp. It's a small, forgettable place with a town hall, a few stores…and not much else.*

India knew that was how most people would see where she lived, but to her it was perfect. She liked how quiet it was, and the frothy vanilla milkshakes at Gracie's Café, and Mrs. O'Donnell's Bakery, with her famous blueberry cheesecake. But what made Yungabilla *really* special was the people, especially in the last few years, when the drought drove families off the land and forced businesses to close down.

When anyone was having a hard time, a neighbor would knock at the door with a dish of lasagna or the community association would come around to fix a broken fence or the whole town would gather under the stars for a movie projected onto the side of the town hall. That made everyone feel better, for a while at least.

India felt at home in Yungabilla, and that's where she was going to stay.

She shook the image of Philomena from her head and snuggled farther into her blankets. She tried again to sleep when she remembered her family staring at her in their small, squished living room, their hopeful faces all wanting her to say yes.

And the hardest memory of all was Dad's disappointed look when he sank back on the couch after she'd said no. It'd been a tough few years, with Boo being sick, Mom quitting her job at school to homeschool him, and Nanna Flo moving in. Then Dad had lost his job when the local newspaper shut down. He'd started a handyman business called Arnie the Fixer. He was contacted at all times of the day and night and often came home with a bandaged thumb or covered in mud or cobwebs. He wasn't a bad handyman or even especially clumsy, but his mind would often wander while he worked. He'd be fixing a drainpipe or unblocking a toilet and start thinking about his days at the newspaper. He'd remember uncovering mischief, like the time the bowling club's chicken mascot was kidnapped or interviewing people who'd done a good deed.

Those were his favorite stories.

He'd written about Daryl, his best friend, who rescued a puppy from the roof of the elementary school after it had been swept up there by a dust storm, and Beryl, who ran over fifty yards in her slippers and nightgown to stop a runaway baby carriage just before it hit the railway tracks.

India knew Dad missed those days, but he hadn't complained or lost his temper—and he never gave up. Not once.

It'd been a long time since the Wimple family had had anything to look forward to. Would it be that bad to stand onstage and spell? Was India being selfish not to even try? Every time Dad suggested it, his face lifted into a huge smile, and it reminded her of how long it had been since she'd seen him that happy. It was a smile she desperately wanted to see again, and if that meant entering the Stupendously Spectacular Spelling Bee to make it happen, it would be worth it.

India made what could only be called a valorous decision.

It was then that Dad popped his head into her room. He did this every night, checking on Boo and India one final time before he went to bed. He leaned over, kissed her on the forehead, and whispered, "Nighty night. Sleep tight."

But as he stood to leave, India said, "I'll do it. I'll sign up for the next spelling bee."

And there it was—the smile. Again.

Dad sat beside her. "Are you sure, sweetheart? I won't let you do anything you don't want to."

"I'm sure," she said, trying to sound as sure as she could.

Dad's face lifted into an even more dazzling smile, but then he did something he absolutely wasn't supposed to do, something that India hadn't counted on at all.

He started crying.

"Dad? Are you OK?"

"Yes," he blubbered. "I'm just so happy." Then he blubbered some more.

"You don't *seem* happy."

"Oh, but I am." He wiped his sleeve across his teary face. "Really."

"There are a few conditions," India said.

"Anything."

"I'll need help practicing."

"We'll start first thing tomorrow."

"And I'll need the whole family with me. It's the only way I'm going to be able to do it."

"Try and keep us away."

"And there's one more thing."

"What's that?"

"I'll need lots of Dad hugs."

"Well, that's lucky, because I have plenty to spare." He held her close. Being wrapped in Dad's hug was one of India's favorite places; she felt as if nothing could ever go wrong when she was there.

"You'd better get some sleep!" Dad sprang to his feet in a way he hadn't sprung for years. "We've got a spelling bee to win."

4

ENDEAVOR

(verb):

Attempt, strive, make an effort.

She endeavored to give it her best shot.

"LADIES AND GENTLEMEN." BOO WAS sitting at a small table covered with the Wimples' best tablecloth. "Welcome to the mock spelling bee trial for champion speller India Wimple."

From the sofa, Mom, Dad, and Nanna Flo cheered.

"Here's how the trial will work." Boo held up a small notebook. "I will read out specially selected words, India will answer them correctly—as she always does—and we will stand back in awe of how brilliant she is."

There were more cheers. The Wimples could be very excitable.

"India?" Boo asked. "Are you ready?"

A mop had been wedged into Dad's toolbox as a pretend microphone. India tightened her ponytail. "Yes."

"Go, India!" Dad called from the audience.

"Quiet please," Boo said in a stern, principal-type voice. "Our champion needs to concentrate. India, here is your first word." He looked at his notebook and read, "*Jocular.* This means comical or humorous. *My jocular uncle is very funny.*"

Ordinarily, if India had been lying on the floor next to Boo, watching the spelling bee on TV, she would have simply spelled the word without missing a beat, but standing in the living room, behind a mop microphone, it wasn't so easy. She wrote the word on her palm with her finger.

She frowned, not sure she had it right, and wrote it again.

"You can do it, honey," Dad whispered.

India took a deep breath and endeavored to answer. "Jocular. J-o-c..." She thought about it some more. "J-o-c...k...u-l-a-r."

Boo checked his notebook, even though he already knew the answer. "I'm afraid that's...incorrect. The correct spelling is j-o-c-u-l-a-r."

"Don't worry, sweetheart," Mom said. "You're just warming up."

"You OK?" Boo asked.

"I'm a little nervous," India admitted.

"No need to be nervous, honey," Nanna Flo said. "You're with family."

"I know, but the real spelling bee will be in front of strangers."

"We'll be there too," Mom said. "Every step of the way."

"I'm sure I'll be fine," India said, not really sounding sure at all.

"Of course you will." Now Dad was sounding unsure too.

"Absolutely," Nanna Flo said. "Those other kids might as well give up."

Now they were all saying things they weren't so sure about.

"This next word is one of your favorites." Boo paused dramatically, just as Philomena would have done. "*Scintillating*. This is an adjective meaning witty or clever. *She had a scintillating way with words.*"

India winced and shifted from one foot to the other, as if her shoes were suddenly too tight. "Scintillating," she repeated shakily. She wrote on her palm. She stopped and started again. "S-i-n…s-i-n-t-a… No, wait. S-c-i…" India dropped her hands to her side. "I'm sorry, Dad. I think this is a bad idea."

"But you know these words," Boo insisted. "They're from the last bee, and you spelled every one of them correctly."

Then Mom stepped in. "Let's try something I did with my students when they were nervous." When Mom used to teach at Yungabilla Elementary School, she was an expert at helping nervous kids relax. "First, I'd ask them to smile. It's a way of tricking your brain into feeling calm."

India tried to smile, but her expression came out crooked and tense.

Mom soldiered on. "Then I asked them to say, 'I'm excited.'"

"Did it work?" India was doubtful.

"Most of the time."

"So I just have to smile and say, 'I'm excited'?"

"Yes, but say it like you really mean it."

"I'm excited," India said without much excitement at all.

"And again."

"I'm excited," she said with a little more excitement.

"That's it!" Dad said, getting a tad excited himself.

"I'm excited!"

Mom was right. India *was* starting to feel better.

"That's the way," Dad cried. "When you're standing in front of that audience, they'll never notice how scared you really are."

India's smile and excitement left her for the far more familiar feeling of sheer terror.

"Oh dear," Dad said.

"I'm sorry," India apologized, "but when I think of standing onstage in front of all those people, I start to feel sick."

"Well, that's no good," Mom decided. "We'll go back to watching it on TV, and you can be our champion at home."

"I really thought I could do it," India said softly.

Dad wrapped her in one of his hugs. "There's nothing to be sorry about. I'm as proud of you as the first time I held you in my arms. Prouder, even."

India snuggled into Dad, closed her eyes, and tried to ignore the voice in her head that kept telling her she'd failed.

5

PERSPICACIOUS

(adjective):

Perceptive, smart, canny.

He had a perspicacious plan he hoped would work.

DAD HAD A PLAN. A *perspicacious* one. Even though he'd have to think hard about how to spell it, he had no doubt that it was perspicacious.

The next Saturday, while Boo and Mom were at a doctor appointment and Nanna Flo was at her judo class, Dad asked India to help him with a job.

"The roof in the town hall needs fixing, and I said I'd take a look. How'd you like to come along?"

India held a spoonful of cereal in the air. "Will we make it back before Boo and Mom come home?"

India always liked to be there when Boo got back from the doctor to know what she'd said.

"Um...sure."

India thought there was something sneaky about his answer. "Really?"

"Yep." Dad grabbed the spoon from her hand and dropped it in the bowl with sudden urgency. "Let's go."

They drove to the hall in Dad's battered van. On the doors of his van he'd painted a sign that read:

ARNIE THE FIXER

YOU BUST IT, I FIX IT

Dad talked steadily all the way there—about the weather, his work, and a low-flying pigeon he suddenly found fascinating. In fact, he spoke almost nonstop, which was something he only did when he was nervous or excited.

"Are you OK, Dad?"

"OK? Of course I'm OK! Never felt better."

He kept talking all the way to the hall and right up to the front doors, but when he flung them open, India's nerves were instantly on high alert. Inside, she saw rows of chairs filled with people.

"What's going on?" she asked.

Dad hoisted his workbag over his shoulder. "A few of the gang said they'd help me out."

He took a step forward, but India tugged his sleeve. "All these people are going to help you fix the roof?"

"Not the roof *exactly*. There's another problem I need help with." He winked. "Come on."

"But I..."

Dad didn't hear because he was already whistling his way to the front of the hall. India wanted to sneak back to the van before anyone noticed her—which, unfortunately, was when Dad's best friend, Daryl, did just that.

"India's here!" Daryl jumped up from his seat and waddled over, pulling on the hood of what was—India blinked to make sure she was seeing right—a onesie cow costume. He threw out his arms. "How do I look?"

"Like a... cow?" India frowned.

The rest of the crowd was pulling on hoods too, and it was only then that India noticed they were *all* dressed in costumes. There were chickens, pandas, frogs, even a peacock.

"What's going on, Daryl?"

"I had a conversation with your dad about how smart you are at spelling—"

"Which is true," Dad called before he ducked behind the stage curtain.

"And we wanted to let you know that Yungabilla is right behind you." Daryl had a big, booming voice, which he always used, including now...when India wished he wouldn't.

"Thank you." She kept her voice low, hoping he'd take the hint. "But the problem isn't my spelling. It's my—"

"Nerves!" he boomed. "We know. Your dad told us. That's why we thought we'd try another practice session."

"Another *practice*?" India felt faint. "We tried that at home and—"

"But you didn't have *us*. This time when you get nervous, just look up and see how ridiculous we look. It will take your mind off your nerves."

The crowd of fluffy humans nodded.

"We're here for you, India." A large parrot, who looked like Mrs. O'Donnell from the bakery, flapped her wings.

India waved back and whispered to Daryl, "Thank you, that's very nice of you, but I—"

"Don't thank us yet. There's more!" Daryl pointed his hoof toward the stage. "Take it away, Arnie!"

The Stupendously Spectacular Spelling Bee theme music blasted from the hall speakers. The curtains flew aside, and onstage, beneath a giant hand-painted banner that read *Spelling Bee*, were Mom, Nanna Flo, and Ernie, sitting at a large desk.

Boo stood at a podium in an oversize sparkly blue suit. "Ladies and gentlemen," he said into the microphone with the flair of a circus ringmaster. "I'd like to introduce you to Yungabilla's candidate for the Stupendously Spectacular Spelling Bee: India Wimple!"

The audience cheered, squawked, and mooed.

India's skin tingled even more, and she wondered why the room suddenly started to spin.

Daryl held out his arm. "Ready for your big moment?"

India desperately wanted to say no and run from the hall, but Daryl hooked his hoof around her arm before she could move. He led her past the furry crowd and onto the stage beside Dad, who was now dressed in a crocodile costume.

Everyone quieted down.

"India Wimple," Daryl boomed, "we in this hall would like to make a few declarations to one of our favorite families in Yungabilla and one of my favorite little girls."

India could feel her face turn a fiery red.

Daryl pulled a folded piece of paper from his pocket and held one hoof on his heart. The audience did the same with their paws, flippers, and wings.

Daryl began: "We declare we will support you in your attempt to be the next Stupendously Spectacular Spelling Bee champion."

"*We do!*" the audience cried.

"Because we think you're brilliant."

"*It's true!*"

"And we will happily wear these costumes for as long as it takes to do it."

"*We will!*"

"This is our declaration to you here today."

"*Hear, hear.*"

"What do you say?" Dad asked, hope all over his face. "You want to give it another try?"

An expectant hush fell over the hall. India recognized even more faces. There was old Joe Miller the butcher, Gracie Hubbard from the café, and kids from school, all staring at her with looks of anticipation.

India hadn't stood in front of so many people since that day when she froze onstage.

She shivered at the thought of it, but despite what she knew she should do, India found herself nodding. "OK."

"That's my girl!" Dad shouted. "Let the spelling bee begin!"

Cries and hoots erupted as Dad gave India one last hug before he and Daryl left the stage and took their seats in the front row.

India scowled at her brother. "I thought you were at the doctor's."

Boo shrugged. "We lied, but it was for a very good cause."

India looked back at the audience settling into their seats, waiting to hear her spell. She felt a wave of sickness and whispered, "I don't think I can do it."

Boo smiled at his sister. "India, you know you're my favorite person in the world, and I mean this in the nicest possible way, but you're wrong. You're amazing, and we want the world to know it."

"You bet your sweet patootie!" Nanna Flo said, even though India wasn't sure what a *patootie* was.

"And remember," Mom said, wearing an exaggerated grin, "a smile will make you feel better!"

India tried, but her face looked more like she'd just stubbed her toe. She would definitely need more practice to get it right.

The crowd fell into an eager silence.

"India," Boo said. "Your first word is *embarrassed*. This is an adjective meaning to be self-conscious or shy."

At that moment, Daryl stood up in his cow suit.

"If I were to use it in a sentence," Boo continued, "I could say, *Daryl was embarrassed when he tripped in front of his friends.*"

Daryl strolled in front of the audience, swinging his tail, until he fell in a spectacular, hoof-waving tumble. The audience laughed.

India smiled briefly before trying to focus on the word.

"Embarrassed," she began. "E-m-b..." She seemed to lose track and began writing on her hand. "E-m-b..."

She paused and then looked up at the costumed audience. India was surprised: it did make her feel better.

She began again with a little more confidence. "E-m-b-a-r-r-a-s-s-e-d. Embarrassed."

"That is correct!" Boo cried.

Nanna Flo rang a cowbell with gusto and shouted, "Yee-haw!" The audience went wild, but this time they pulled posters from underneath their seats that read, "You can do it, India!" and, "Go, India!"

There was even a sign that said, "India for Prime Minister."

"Your next word," Boo said, suddenly serious, "is *songstress*. This is a noun meaning a female singer."

A woman in a koala suit stood up. India couldn't be certain, but she thought it looked a lot like her teacher.

"Mrs. Wild?" she asked.

"Hello, dear." She waved her paw. "When your dad asked if we could help you get over your jitters, we were happy to. Weren't we?" She turned to the costumed crowd around her, which India now realized were the kids from her class.

"You can do it, India!"

Boo continued. "If I used it in a sentence, I could say, *Mrs. Wild is a wonderful teacher, but sadly, she's a terrible songstress.*"

Mrs. Wild burst into a high-pitched, operatic squeal. The audience plugged their ears and groaned. Some even fell to the floor.

India giggled. "Songstress. S-o-n-g-s-t-r-e-s-s. Songstress."

"That is correct!" Boo declared.

Nanna Flo rang the cowbell. "I knew you'd nail it!"

Boo read out more words. Audience members sprang from their seats to help act out each one. There was Hector, the policeman; Lois and Edna, the grocery store owners; and Ahmed, the bus driver—all here just for her. Gradually, India felt more at ease, almost as if she were in her living room on a Friday night.

The words became harder, but India didn't flinch, right up until Boo's very last word. "*Aficionado,*" he said carefully. "This is a noun meaning a person who is very knowledgeable about an activity or subject. *India was a spelling bee aficionado.*"

India looked straight into the audience, each of their hooded faces willing her to get it right. "Aficionado. A-f-i-c-i-o-n-a-d-o. Aficionado."

"Correct-o-mundo!"

Nanna Flo rang her cowbell in one continuous *clang-lang-lang*.

"Ladies and gentlemen," Boo announced, "India has spelled fifty words without one mistake."

The crowd sprang to their feet, cheering and hugging each other in a wild animal rumpus.

Dad scrambled onto the stage, his tail flopping behind him, and knelt before India. "So what do you think? Would you like to give the competition a try?"

"Do you really think I can do it?"

"I *know* you can do it," Dad said. "We all do. You just have to convince yourself."

A town hall filled with friends and family was one thing, but could she be onstage, in front of an audience of strangers, with cameras broadcasting her face into the living rooms of millions of people?

Even thinking about it made her dizzy.

"Will you, India?" Daryl asked, straightening his cow horns that had drooped a little to the side. "Anytime you get nervous, just think of us."

A gathering of birds, frogs, and bears stood beside Daryl and nodded their costumed heads. India had known most of them all her life. Each one was there just for her, waiting for her decision.

Even though being in front of a crowd normally made her feel queasy and scared, India realized she didn't feel *completely* terrified, and that's why she answered, "OK."

This time, there was no stopping them. Everyone in the hall was dancing and throwing their wings and paws in the air.

Nanna Flo and Mom joined in the hugging, while Boo simply smiled at his sister. "See?" he asked. "You're amazing, just like I said."

For the first time since that Friday night in front of the TV, India thought she might—*just might*—have a chance of being the next Stupendously Spectacular Spelling Bee champion.

6

TREPIDATION

(noun):

Fear, apprehension, the heebie-jeebies.

She lay awake most of the night, full of trepidation.

DAD'S PLAN HAD WORKED.

After facing the audience of friends in their finest costumes, India's nerves had settled down and preparations for the Spelling Bee began in earnest. The Wimple family helped her practice, just as Dad had promised. The first round was only a few weeks away, and he drew up a plan, so every spare second was devoted to spelling.

They practiced over dinner and breakfast and on the way to school, and Mrs. Wild made sure to have extra spelling games in class every day. India's favorite way to practice was bouncing on the trampoline while Boo sat in a chair calling out words. With each jump, she had to say another letter, without missing a bounce.

She also loved when they'd lie on the picnic blanket in the

backyard and Mom would tell them stories, stopping at unexpected moments for India to spell the last word she'd said.

Her favorite story was one Mom made up called "Brave Boo and Ingenious India," about two courageous children who fought *villainous* baddies and *ravenous* monsters. Mom would throw in as many difficult words as she could, and India would spell them all.

Perfectly.

While she was at school, Nanna Flo, Boo, and Mom would stick words on the fridge, along the hall, on her bedroom ceiling, even on the back of the bathroom door, so that the whole house was wallpapered with words.

In the mornings, Nanna Flo, who was an early riser, would sneak into India's room, lean in only inches away from her granddaughter's face, and wait for her to wake up.

When India woke to see Nanna's giant eyes staring down at her, she'd squeal.

"Morning, sunshine," Nanna Flo would say. "Ready to spell?"

It was something India never quite got used to.

At night, Mom, Dad, and Boo would practice with her until none of them could hold in their yawns any longer. They'd say good night, and Dad would switch on the night-light in the hall, which sent a faint beam linking Boo's room with India's.

"Night, Boo," India whispered.

"Night, India," Boo whispered right back.

India would slip under the blankets, sneak her flashlight from her bedside drawer, and flick through the dictionary to choose the hardest words she could find.

Pertinacious.

Tenacious.

Temerarious.

When Dad crept in to check on India, he often found her asleep, head resting on the dictionary, the creased pages making lines on her cheek. Dad would carefully slip the book out from under her head and settle her back onto the pillow.

Roused from sleep, she'd groan and mumble more words: "*Camouflage, fluorescent, slumberous.*"

"That's right, sweetheart. Now it's time to sleep."

When she heard Dad's voice and felt his kiss on her head, she'd finally fall into a deep, wordless slumber.

But the night before the first round of the spelling bee was different. The house had long settled into sleep, but even Dad's voice hadn't worked, and India was still awake. She stared at the luminous, green numbers on her alarm clock.

3:23.

She worried about being with the other kids, about whether she would freeze in front of the crowd, if she'd even be able to spell her own name. What if she just wasn't good enough?

3:45.

She tried to make herself drift off by quietly reciting words, but every time she promised herself it would be the last one, her brain jumped to another: *punctilious, perseverant, persistent.*

4:15.

Fatigued.

Weary.

Exhausted.

Until…

A small, muffled cough drifted across the hall, and India was instantly awake.

She leaped from her bed and into Boo's room. She found him

slumped forward and short of breath. His shoulders rose and fell in waves, and he was gasping for breath.

India grabbed his blue inhaler and gave it a shake before popping on the spacer.

"Sorry," Boo said between strangled breaths. "For waking you."

"Don't be silly." India handed him the inhaler. "I couldn't sleep. At least this way I get to be useful."

By now everyone was up—disheveled and rumpled but fully awake—just as they always were when Boo needed them at night.

When Boo had a flare-up, it usually started with a quiet whistling. Each time he took a breath, it sounded as if someone were sitting on his chest, crushing all the air out of him, making it hard to breathe. Then came the coughing.

Mom sat by Boo's side. India pressed another puff of medication into the spacer, and the Wimples silently counted each of his four breaths.

"That's it, honey," Mom said. "You'll feel better any minute now." She was an expert at sounding calm when Boo had a flare-up.

Dad stood behind them, silent and still. He wasn't as good as Mom at hiding how scared he was. Nanna Flo linked her arm through Dad's. "Your mom's right," she said. "You'll be good as new in no time."

Everyone knew she said it more for Dad than Boo.

Last year had been especially bad for Boo, and this was the main reason Mom had left her job, so she could be near him during the day—*in case*.

She never said in case of what, and the rest of the Wimples were happy that she never did.

Mom gently stroked his back, still using her same calm voice. "Nice, steady breaths."

They could never tell what would trigger a flare-up. It could be running, laughing, smoke, or dust. Sometimes it seemed to be nothing at all.

What the Wimple family *did* know was that these were the scariest times of their lives.

Slowly, Boo was able to fill his lungs, and the feeling of his chest being squished finally eased.

"I'm OK now."

And just like that, every uptight shoulder in the Wimple family relaxed.

"We knew you'd be fine," Dad said, even though he hadn't believed it until right then. He gave Boo one of his Dad hugs, one that lasted a little longer than usual, and tucked him in. "Would you like me to stay?"

"I'll stay," India said. "Just until Boo falls asleep."

India often did this after a flare-up. She did it to make sure Boo really *was* OK, but Dad also knew it was to send away the worried thoughts in her head that would grow bigger if she went to bed right away.

"OK," Dad said, "but not for long. We've got a spelling bee to get to."

Boo held up his blankets and India climbed in beside him.

"Are you sure you feel OK?" she asked.

"Much better." His voice was scratchy. "Tell me a story."

"Which one?" India didn't really need to ask—she knew exactly what he'd say.

"The story of when I was born," he whispered.

"OK." They nestled in closer and India began. "When Mom told me she was having a baby, I screamed and danced around the kitchen for five whole minutes, but when she said we'd have to wait six months, I sat down on the floor and cried. We counted down, marking off every day on the calendar, but it still felt as if you'd never get here. Then, you came six weeks early. It happened so fast, Mom thought you'd be born in the back of Dad's car. Nanna Flo said you were in a hurry because you couldn't wait to meet us."

"Then what happened?" He knew the answer but he asked anyway.

"The doctors told us your lungs were too small and that you might not make it. Nanna Flo said, 'Fiddlesticks! He's a Wimple, and we Wimples never give up! He's going to be just fine.'"

"The doctor showed us into the nursery. You were in a plastic crib, crying and covered in all these wires and tubes that were attached to a machine that groaned and hissed beside you. The nurses said you weren't strong enough to breathe on your own, so the machine was doing it for you."

"What did I look like?"

"You were wrinkly and purple. But when we were finally allowed to see you, you stopped crying, as if you'd been crying out for *us*, and when I reached through the small, round window to touch you, you grabbed my finger. The doctors said you were weak, but you squeezed my finger so hard it was sore for days."

"That's not true."

"It is, and I had the bruises to prove it! I knew then that no matter what the doctors said, you weren't going anywhere."

"Except to bed." Dad poked his head around the door. "Because I need to make sure my champion spelling team has enough sleep."

India slipped out of bed and carefully fixed the blankets beneath Boo's chin. "Night, Boo," she whispered.

"Night, India," Boo whispered right back.

India crossed the hall to her room, leaving her door open, as she always did, to let the glow from the night-light connect Boo's room to hers.

7

PRECARIOUS

(noun):

Uncertain, unsettled, a little rocky.

What seemed like a good idea suddenly felt very precarious.

INDIA FELT AS IF SHE'D only been asleep for a few minutes when the house rang with alarm clocks, and she woke on the floor beside Boo. This sometimes happened when she worried about him. She never remembered going there, just waking up beside him.

"How do you feel?" she asked.

"Fantastic," Boo said.

The wheezing was there, lurking behind every word he said.

"We don't have to go if you're not up to it."

Boo threw off his blankets. "No offense, India, but it took a lot of work to get you here. There's no way I'm letting you back out now. Plus, I feel fine, like I said."

India scowled. "You're a terrible liar."

"No I'm not. I'm Brave Boo, who fights *merciless* monsters and is about to escort his *preposterously* smart sister into one of the most *tremendous* moments of her life."

"As long as I don't pass out or throw up."

"You won't," Boo said with a grin. "You'll be fine. As your little brother, I know."

The house filled with the chaos of getting ready and last-minute spelling drills over breakfast. Mom made sandwiches and packed drinks for the trip, while Dad sang in the shower at the top of his voice.

He was happy—happier than he'd been in a long time.

The rest of the house would have been happier if Dad were a better singer.

When they were all ready, they scrambled out the door.

But something was missing…or some*one*.

"Where's Nanna Flo?" Dad looked at his watch.

"In her bedroom," Mom said. "She needed a few more minutes to get ready."

"*Ready*?" Dad's face reddened, which also happened when he got nervous. "All she has to do is put in her teeth and she's done. How long does that take?"

Nanna finally appeared at the door.

"She's got Ernie," Mom sighed as Nanna hobbled toward them.

"The van's pretty crowded," Dad said as gently as he could. "Do you think we really need to bring Ernie along?"

"Of course we do! Who will protect me if I leave him behind?"

Sometimes Nanna Flo said things that didn't make much sense. This was one of those times.

Nanna squished into the back seat next to India. She sat Ernie on her lap and clicked the seat belt around them both. "If we don't leave now, we're going to be late," she scolded Dad.

"Yes, Ma."

After a few choked rumbles, the van finally kicked to life.

"Ready, Team Wimple?" Dad called over his shoulder.

"Ready!" the Wimples cried.

Dad shifted the van into gear, and with a noisy sputter, they were on their way.

"And we're off!" Dad said. "On the road to India's championship run."

"Honey." No one could mistake the warning tone in Mom's voice. "You said you wouldn't be too—"

"I know, I'm sorry," Dad apologized. "We can't get our hopes up too much. It's going to be a tough competition." He paused before adding, "But I can't help it if our daughter was born to spell."

Dad knew from Mom's expression that he'd said the wrong thing again.

"I think what your father means"—Mom poked her head

between the seats—"is that we're proud of you, India, no matter what happens."

"Of course. That's exactly what I meant." Dad looked into the rearview mirror and gave India a wink.

"Thanks, Dad, but thousands of kids will be trying to get through this first round. What are the chances of me being one of them?"

"Pretty good, I'd say, or you can sprinkle me with pepper and roast me for dinner," Nanna Flo said. "In fact, someone oughta tell those other kids they're wasting their time because India Wimple is coming!"

Mom sighed, the van backfired, and Nanna Flo cuddled Ernie into her lap.

~

The first round of the spelling bee was held in a small town called Dunnydoon, over an hour's drive away. When Dad pulled the van into the parking lot of the town hall, the area was alive with nervous kids and their parents.

The Wimples piled out, and Dad took a deep, ready-for-battle breath. "Here we are—the first round. How do you feel, India?"

When India didn't reply, the Wimples looked around and realized that, well, she was gone.

"India?" Dad scanned the parking lot, but it was Boo who spotted her first.

"I think she's over there."

A pair of red sneakers was poking out from behind a Dumpster.

The Wimples crept toward the container and found India sitting on the ground. Her auburn hair looked even darker against her deathly white face.

"Are you OK?" Dad asked.

"I thought I'd sit for a while."

"Yeah." Dad nodded to the others. "Good idea."

The Wimples sat on the ground beside her.

Dad held her hand. "You don't have to do this. If you decide to walk away now, no one will think any less of you."

Dad's voice made her feel calmer.

"I'm OK." And she almost meant it.

"The important thing is not to be scared," Dad said, even though he sounded a little scared too.

"It's true." Nanna Flo was doing that thing where she was looking at India but was mostly talking to Dad. "Especially when you've got family who'd do anything for you." She turned up her nose. "Even sit next to a Dumpster that smells like the back end of a cow."

India smiled for the first time that morning.

But she still didn't move.

So they sat some more.

"While we're breathing in this beautiful aroma, I might as well tell a story," Nanna Flo said. "When I was young, I sang at all the weddings in Yungabilla and at church on Sundays. Everyone said I had the voice of an angel. One time after mass, a man showed me his card and invited me to audition for the Sydney Opera Company."

"You never told me you sang at the Sydney Opera House," Dad said.

"I didn't tell you," Nanna Flo said sheepishly, "because I didn't go."

"Why not?" India asked.

"I was too scared. I thought I wouldn't be good enough. And now I'm an old lady and I've never even been *inside* the opera house." She sighed. "There's still this little part of me, all these years later, that wonders what would have happened if I'd gone."

"I bet you would have been great!" India said.

"Yes, but we'll never know."

India took a deep breath. "I'm still kind of scared."

"It's only natural," Nanna Flo said. "All great moments in life are worth a couple of nerves. So, what do you think? We keep sitting with the garbage or go inside?"

"Let's go inside."

"I was hoping you'd say that," Nanna Flo sniffed, "because I was about to pass out from the s-t-i-n-k."

8

CALAMITOUS

(adjective):

Disastrous, catastrophic, or really, really bad.

Despite her preparation, the whole attempt felt calamitous.

THE WIMPLES BRUSHED THEMSELVES OFF and walked through the crowded parking lot toward the hall.

When they entered the lobby, there were even more people.

And they were everywhere.

India's heart flipped, and she thought she was going to faint, which of course made her worry even more. If she collapsed on the floor, she'd embarrass herself before she'd even stepped onstage.

Her toe caught the edge of the carpet, and she stumbled through the door. Dad caught her before she fell. "I've got you."

Mom grabbed her other arm. "Me too."

After registering with the spelling bee officials, India was given a large, numbered card to hang around her neck, and the Wimples were directed inside a bustling auditorium. Film crews adjusted lights and interviewed feverish contestants. India hid behind her family and made herself as small as possible, so none of the cameras would point her way.

Onstage, two officials sat at a table. One was a slumped-over bald man with a mustache that sat over his lip like a fluffy caterpillar. Beside him was a woman wearing a black skirt and jacket with tall, black boots and a scowl that was just as dark. Her hair was pulled back into a tight, orderly bun. She tapped a sharp fingernail against her microphone to quiet the audience.

It didn't work.

"Ladies and gentlemen." She had a clipped way of speaking that reminded India of whips being cracked.

The audience kept fussing. Some became even rowdier.

She frowned, took a deep breath, and bellowed, "Will you all be quiet!"

The audience froze in an immediate hush.

"That's better." She eyed the crowd as if daring them to make a sound. "I am Ms. Hatchet, the pronouncer for today's round, and my colleague Mr. Spratt will keep the time and score."

She pointed at the rows of chairs onstage. "Contestants, you must now go to your allocated seats and all family members will sit down there." She pointed into the hall as if she were shooing a grubby child from the room.

It was hard to tell whether India or Dad was more nervous.

"We can't sit together?" Dad looked as if he wasn't going to move until Mom took his arm.

"Not if we don't want to upset Ms. Hatchet." She kissed India on the forehead. "Good luck, and remember to smile."

India tried once again, but it came out all wrong, like she was about to be horribly sick.

"Wait! I almost forgot." Nanna Flo pulled a hanky from inside her sleeve. "I wanted to give you this."

"Thanks, Nanna, but I already have a hanky."

"This is no ordinary hanky—it's the Wimple family's lucky hanky. My mother gave it to my father before he went to the war, and he said it was the reason he returned home in one piece."

"Do you think that's true?" India asked.

"Father believed it, and I think he would enjoy that it's coming in handy again."

"Thanks, Nanna." India tucked the hanky into her pocket.

Nanna Flo patted Ernie's head. "Ernie thinks you're going to be fine too."

"Good-luck hug?" Boo asked.

"Yes, please."

"You'll be great, sis," he whispered. "I know it."

India climbed the stairs onto the stage, concentrating the whole time on not tripping. When she took her seat beside the other kids, she kept her head down, trying not to make eye contact, worried that someone might turn around at any moment and say hello.

Her stomach fluttered just thinking about it.

"Children and parents," Ms. Hatchet barked, "welcome to the first round of the Stupendously Spectacular Spelling Bee."

Even though she'd said *welcome,* it sounded anything *but* welcoming.

"Today, thousands of children all around the country are battling for their place in the grand final. These are knockout rounds. Each child who spells a word incorrectly will be... *eliminated.*"

India shuddered at the way Ms. Hatchet seemed to enjoy saying "eliminated."

"The last contestant to spell a word correctly will proceed to round two. Let's begin."

India suddenly felt hot, as if someone had turned up the heat.

Her mouth became dry. She wondered how long a dehydrated body could survive before it simply collapsed.

She didn't have long to think about it before Ms. Hatchet called the first contestant, Harry Harrison.

The small, thin boy walked to the microphone at the front of the stage. His shorts and shirt were so big that India thought he must've dressed in someone else's clothes by mistake.

Ms. Hatchet pronounced the first word. "*Devour.* This is a verb that means to gobble, guzzle, or feast."

She had a small, devouring smile.

India spelled the word in her head.

The boy took a deep breath and began. "Devour. D-e-v-o-u-r. Devour."

Everyone in the room held their breath until Ms. Hatchet announced, without a trace of joy, "That is correct."

Harry smiled with relief and hurried back to his seat.

India watched as more kids were called. Some tall, some short, some confident, and some who looked downright terrified.

Then it was her turn.

Her heart did another flip—a really big one this time—and beat so wildly she worried it might be too much and just give up altogether.

She looked at the microphone. It seemed an infinitely long way away. She carefully lifted each foot, trying desperately to ignore the fact that everyone in the room was staring directly at her.

She attempted a smile, knowing it probably looked all wrong, when the voice inside her head came back. *This is crazy. This is ridiculous. Even thinking you can win is completely…*

"*Calamitous.*"

India looked up, worried that Ms. Hatchet had read her thoughts.

"This is an adjective meaning devastating, catastrophic"—the pronouncer paused and gave India a steely glare—"or very, very disastrous."

India gulped.

She knew this one by heart, she was sure of it. She just had to stay calm.

But then it happened—the same feeling she'd had during the school play. She felt frozen to the stage and her body trembled with waves of fear.

The words she'd practiced, every word she knew, began to disappear from her memory, like fireworks fizzing out to nothing, leaving behind a black, empty space.

Mr. Spratt rang a small bell. "Thirty seconds remaining."

India panicked. She tried to open her mouth, but her teeth clamped shut. Her breathing grew short. She felt dizzy.

I knew this would happen, the voice said. *It* is *calamitous, just like last time when you—*

India looked up to drive the voice away and to search for the quickest way out of the auditorium…but then she saw the Wimples, sitting in a row, smiling at her and all wearing animal beanies.

Almost instantly, the room stopped spinning and the word slowly began to reappear. She wrote it on her palm just to be sure. She checked and double-checked.

"Ten seconds," Mr. Spratt warned.

India took a deep breath. "Calamitous. C-a-l-a-m-i-t-o-u-s. Calamitous."

Ms. Hatchet leaned into her microphone. A small, down-turned crease in her lip seemed to suggest she was disappointed. "That is correct."

The Wimples leaped from their seats and let out cheers and hoots. The people around them stared.

Ms. Hatchet was not impressed. "The audience will refrain from noisy outbursts."

Dad waved a small, apologetic wave, and they all sat down.

I did it, India kept thinking all the way back to her seat. *I did it.*

More kids made their way to the microphone and more words were called.

Hesitant.

Introverted.

Acquiescent.

India's next attempt went more smoothly.

"Ingenious," Ms. Hatchet announced. "This is an adjective meaning resourceful, intelligent, or talented."

India thought back to Mom's stories of Ingenious India, and this time her smile came with almost no effort at all.

"Ingenious. I-n-g-e-n-i-o-u-s. Ingenious."

"That is correct."

More spellers came and went. Many were asked to leave the stage after they'd misspelled their word. Some went quietly, shaking their heads. Others fled in an outburst of tears.

The chairs around India emptied until there was only herself and Harry Harrison left.

Harry was up first.

"*Precipice,*" Ms. Hatchet said. "This is a noun meaning a cliff face or sheer drop."

Harry moved to the microphone. "Precipice. P-r-e..." He stopped.

India snuck a look at Harry. Until this moment, he'd spelled everything without hesitation.

"...c-i..." He took a hanky from his pocket and wiped his brow.

India spelled the rest of the word in her head, willing him to hear her.

"...p-a-c-e. Precipice."

India felt her heart plunge. This was always the worst part of watching the spelling bee—the moment when she knew a kid's hopes were about to be dashed.

Ms. Hatchet spoke carefully. "That is incorrect."

There were sighs and murmurs of disappointment from the audience.

"The word is spelled p-r-e-c-i-p-i-c-e. If India's next attempt is correct, she will be the winner of today's heat and will advance to the second round in Huddersfield."

The room fell silent as India stepped to the microphone.

"India, your word is *iridescent*. This is an adjective meaning having luminous colors that change when seen from different angles."

India felt her legs tingle. She wrote on her hand to double-check. She was positive that she knew how to spell it.

Are you really positive? the voice asked. *If you get this wrong, you're out for sure.*

She looked up again, eager to ignore the voice. Mom gave one of her biggest, warmest smiles.

"Iridescent. I-r-i-d-e-s-c-e-n-t. Iridescent."

"That is correct," Ms. Hatchet said flatly. "You are going through to the next round."

This time nothing was going to stop the Wimples—not even Ms. Hatchet's brutal stare. They jumped from their seats, whooping and cheering. Nanna Flo put her fingers between her teeth and let out a whistle that echoed around the hall.

India turned to Harry. "You were really good."

"Thanks," he said. "I hope you make it to the finals. Kids from the country never win, but I figure you could."

Dad couldn't help himself. He sprinted down the center of the auditorium, jumped onstage, and swept India into the air.

Ms. Hatchet attempted to stop him. "Mr. Wimple, this is hardly an appropriate way to—"

But she gave up, knowing there was no point once all the other Wimples joined in. India felt light-headed in Dad's arms but wasn't sure if it was the spinning or the simple fact of what had just happened.

She had done it! She was going through to the next round.

And the voice inside her head was completely silent.

9

WORRISOME

(adjective):

Nerve-racking, perturbing, an unsettling feeling.

It was indeed a worrisome turn of events.

AFTER STUMBLING OVER A FEW brief words addressed to the TV cameras and posing for a somewhat awkward photo for the local paper, India was relieved to be back in the family van. The drive was filled with singing, mostly led by Dad's off-key wailing, which, this time, no one really minded.

When they arrived home, somewhat tired and rumpled, the Wimples found the kitchen table filled with food and a note stuck to a jug of freshly made lemonade:

A FEAST FOR A CHAMPION
FROM YOUR FRIENDS IN YUNGABILLA

India's stomach growled at the meal before them: coleslaw,

mashed potatoes, roast chicken, and gravy. And in the center was Mrs. O'Donnell's famous blueberry cheesecake.

"Let's dig in!" Dad said, but all through dinner, India could tell something was bothering him. She knew because he was trying extra hard to look excited, but on his forehead was what Mom called his "worry crease."

"Is anything wrong, Dad?"

"Wrong? No! How could anything be wrong? Today my little girl won her spelling bee."

Dad was a terrible liar.

"Fiddlesticks!" Nanna Flo noticed the worry crease too. "You're fibbing. Tell us what's wrong."

Dad knew there was no point trying to hide it. "Before we left the club, I was given the details of the next round. It's going to be a little costly, that's all. But that's my problem."

"How much money?" Mom asked.

"I'm not sure yet."

"Well, let's figure it out." Nanna Flo pulled a notepad from the kitchen drawer. "What do we need?"

Dad began listing the costs while Nanna Flo wrote it all down—and it added up fast. The next round in Huddersfield was a six-hour drive away, so they'd need to stay overnight. The gas and RV park costs alone were going to be pretty steep.

It really was worrisome.

Mom bit her lip. Boo frowned. Dad kept cranking his head this way and that, as if the numbers would change if he looked at them from a different angle.

But they never did.

"It's just a silly competition," India said. "I can drop out."

"Double fiddlesticks!" Nanna Flo cried, saying what everyone else was thinking. "There's nothing silly about my granddaughter being one of the best spellers the world has ever seen."

"But we can't afford it." India shrugged.

"We'll *find* a way to afford it," Dad said.

But now the whole family had Dad's worry crease, which made him worry even more. Until he made a stand. Literally. He got to his feet and puffed out his chest.

"What does it say on the side of my van?" Dad didn't wait for the answer. "*Arnie the Fixer,* that's what, and I'm going to fix this too."

"How?" Boo asked.

"With a brilliant plan."

"What brilliant plan?"

"I'd tell you, but it's way past your bedtime."

As much as India loved Dad, she thought his answer smelled fishy.

Dad started gathering up the plates. "Off you go. I'll be there soon to tuck you in."

The Wimples knew Dad didn't have a brilliant plan and that he was telling another fib, but this time no one called out *fiddlesticks* because they were quietly hoping it might come true.

It had been a long day by the time India finally climbed into bed. As she listened to Mom's story of Brave Boo and Ingenious India, she tried hard to concentrate as Boo *courageously* battled a three-headed monster and India *concocted* a clever *decoy* to lure the beast away from her *fearless* brother and into an *elaborate* trap.

~~~

That night, India's dreams were filled with swords and ropes and dangling from flying machines when she was woken by a giant crash.

At first she wasn't sure if she'd dreamed the crash until she heard a low groan. Her heart jolted.

"Boo!" She sped across the hall to his room, but he was already out of bed. "You heard it too?"

Mom and Dad appeared next. "Is everyone OK?"

Before they could answer, they heard another groan. It was coming from Nanna Flo's room. Dad got there first and saw her lying on the floor, shards of broken plaster all around her.

And scattered money. Lots of it.
~~~

Dad knelt beside Nanna Flo. "Are you OK?"

"Yes, yes," she insisted. "Just a little embarrassed."

"What happened?" Mom asked.

"I wanted to help India make it to the next round of the competition." She stared at the mess on the floor. "But the plug in Ernie was hard to pull out, and I dropped him."

That's when they all realized the broken pieces of plaster were Ernie.

"Where did you get all this money?" Dad asked.

"I've been saving a little each week from my pension, in case we needed it for a good cause—and I think we have one."

"There must be hundreds of dollars here," Boo said.

"Five hundred and twenty-five to be exact," Nanna Flo said, "which is enough to cover all of us traveling to the next round."

"We'll pay you back," Dad said.

"Fiddlesticks!" Nanna Flo said. "You won't do anything of the kind. I'm part of this family too, and I'd like to help out. What do you say, India? Want to give the next round a shot?"

"I think I would." India sniffed. "Thank you, Nanna."

Nanna Flo wiped the tear that was trembling on India's eyelashes. "You're most welcome, but there are two things I'd like in return."

"Anything," India said.

"I'll need help sweeping up Ernie."

"Of course."

"And can you help me off this floor? My backside's starting to go numb."

10

FORTUITOUS

(adjective):

Unexpected, unanticipated, completely lucky.

It was a fortuitous encounter none of them expected.

"BRAVE BOO STEPPED ONTO THE tattered rope bridge that swung over the gaping chasm."

"C-h-a-s-m," India spelled.

"To the castle of the evil overlord."

It was the morning of the next round, and Mom told the story as she lay on the grass in the backyard with Boo, India, and Nanna Flo beside her.

"The same evil overlord whose flock of vultures had kidnapped Ingenious India, who was now being held prisoner. Even though the overlord was truly malevolent—"

"M-a-l-e-v-o-l-e-n-t."

"—Brave Boo would teach him not to mess with his sister. The bridge swung in the icy updrafts. Brave Boo focused on reaching the castle door ahead, ignoring the frayed rope and the deadly drop beneath him, when, from the blackened skies, a fire-breathing griffin—"

"G-r-i-f-f-i-n."

"—half-lion, half-eagle, swept toward him. Brave Boo held out his sword, ready to defend himself, but the griffin flew straight past him and instead breathed its fiery breath onto the bridge, immediately setting it ablaze.

"Ingenious India saw the flames from her room at the top of the tower. She knew there were only seconds before the bridge would fall, sending Boo plummeting. She had to think of a plan. She had to save her brother. She had to—"

"How do I look?" Dad was standing on the back steps dressed in a lime-green suit. Fred Greenburg had given it to him as payment after Dad fixed his leaking toilet. It was tight around his stomach and a little short in the sleeves and legs.

"You look as dashing as when I first met you," Mom said.

This wasn't exactly true—in fact, it wasn't true at all—but it was something India loved about her mom and dad. Fibbing was allowed in situations like these.

"Let's go then!"

After they'd brushed themselves down, the Wimple family piled into the van. Dad had to turn the key a few times before it sputtered to life and they were off, but they'd only driven a few miles out of Yungabilla when the engine coughed and groaned and the van staggered to a stop by the side of the road.

"I'm sure this won't take long," Dad said, squeezing out of his tight jacket and rolling up his shirtsleeves. He grabbed his toolbox and began working under the hood. There was a series of clangs and grunts and one very loud "Ouch!"

"Are you OK?" Mom called.

"Fine," Dad sang back.

"Huddersfield is a long way." India tried not to sound worried. "Do you think we'll be there on time?"

"Your father will do his best." Mom glanced down at her watch and, for a second, even she wore Dad's worry crease. "We can use the time for a little more practice."

Mom, Boo, and Nanna Flo took turns choosing their favorite tricky words, and Dad finally shouted, "All done!" He appeared from behind the hood, his shirt and face streaked with grease. "She'll need a little bit of a push to get started."

Nanna Flo got out first.

"Not you, Ma," Dad said.

"Why not me?" She flexed her muscles. "I can arm-wrestle you under the table any day."

The Wimple family lined up behind the van while Dad sat

behind the steering wheel. He turned the key, and the engine wheezed and chugged before falling silent.

"OK...and push!"

The Wimples shoved with everything they had, and the van began to move forward. Dad tried again to start the engine. It clunked and whirred.

"That's it!" Dad yelled out the window. "We're moving!"

But it was at that moment three dramatic things happened:

1. The engine sparked to life.
2. The wheels spun in the soggy ground.
3. A shower of mud flew into the air and all over the Wimples.

Dad pulled on the emergency brake, poked his head out the window, and stared at his mud-covered family. "Sorry."

Huge globs of brown gunk dripped from them. They stood in soggy silence until Boo said, "Maybe no one will notice." He wiped away the mud to reveal a smirk that made the others smile too.

"Why are we standing around?" Nanna swiped a splat from her face. "We've got a spelling bee to get to!"

The Wimples dragged their grubby selves into the van, put on their seat belts, and, with a groaning *clang*, Dad shifted into gear and they lumbered back onto the road.

The van shuddered and shook as it drove along the highway. Every other vehicle passed it easily, including a squad of elderly motorcyclists. Dad patted the dashboard. "That's it, girl. Not far now."

As they drove into Huddersfield, Mom read the map and directed Dad through the unfamiliar streets. Nanna Flo glanced at her watch, wondering if they were ever going to make it, when Boo spotted a Stupendously Spectacular Spelling Bee banner. "Over there!"

Once again, the contest was in the town hall—a beautiful stone building with a clock tower that loomed high above.

Dad peeked at the clock. They had two minutes until registration closed. "Get ready to run, Wimples!" He pulled to the curb with a screech of tires.

The Wimples raced up the red-carpeted stairs and beneath the arched doorway. They zigzagged through the crowd in the lobby and followed the spelling bee signs until they stood—muddy, bedraggled, and out of breath—in front of the registration desk.

"We're the Wimples," Dad panted, his teeth shining brightly from his grease-streaked face. "And this is India. She's here to compete."

A teenage girl with bright-blue pigtails was seated beside a rather grouchy-looking man with a hairpiece that looked like a small hamster had settled on his head. The man looked at the Wimples up and down making a face as if a stray dog had just peed on his favorite pair of slippers.

"You're late," he sneered.

"We had some car trouble," Dad explained, "but we're here now, and we're—"

"Too late," the man with the rodent hair said smugly. "Registration has closed."

Dad looked at his watch. "Three minutes ago."

The man smiled in a way that wasn't very friendly. "Which makes you three minutes *late*."

Dad wasn't about to give up. "Maybe you could ignore that since we've come so far and—"

"Ignore the *rules*?" He looked as if Dad had just asked him to swim with sharks. "What is the point of having rules if we simply *ignore* them?"

Nanna Flo jabbed her muddy hands onto her muddy hips. "Because a worn-out van and a puffed-up, pompous official shouldn't get in the way of one of this country's greatest spellers."

"I'm sorry, madam, but rules are rules." He didn't seem sorry at all as he picked up his laptop and strutted away.

"He can't do that." Nanna Flo rolled up her sleeves. "I'm going to teach that miserable man a judo lesson he'll never—"

Dad held her back. "No, Mom. He's right. We're late."

The Wimples stood, slumped over in disappointment, and watched the official leave.

It was only now, after India's chances of registering were gone, that she realized how much she wanted to compete. A teeny-tiny part of her was even excited about standing in front of the microphone again.

Despondent, India thought. *A word meaning being sad or dismayed. D-e-s-p-o-n-d-e-n-t.*

"I'm sorry, India," Dad said. Unlike the rodent-haired man, he meant it all the way to his toes. "I really tried to get us here on time."

"That's OK." India shrugged. "It's just a competition."

Anyone who had been listening could tell from her voice that it wasn't *just* a competition at all.

Luckily for India, there *was* someone listening.

The teenager at the table had been packing up but stopped when she saw the tears glistening in India's eyes.

She wound back her watch and held out her arm. "Look! According to me, it's two minutes *before* registration closes."

"But that man said—" Dad began.

"It doesn't matter what he said." She scowled. "He's been in a bad mood all day. And people say teenagers are grumpy."

"That's the way," Nanna Flo cheered. "I like a little rule bending."

The teenager opened her laptop and found India's name. "Here you are." Her fingers flew across the keys before she handed over a numbered card. "You're in."

"Thank you!" India draped the card around her neck.

"We'll never forget this!" Dad shook the girl's hand so hard that India worried he'd shake it off.

"You're welcome, but you have to hurry. It's about to start."

The Wimples tore across the lobby and slipped into the auditorium only seconds before the doors were closed.

11

SKULDUGGERY

(noun):

Trickery, underhandedness, funny business.

It seemed there was a lot of skulduggery going on.

INSIDE THE TOWN HALL, THE atmosphere was even more tense than the first round in Dunnydoon. The Wimples were directed to the front of the room near the stage, past TV cameras and broods of anxious parents fussing over kids and squeezing in some last-minute spelling drills.

Victorious.

Triumphant.

Celebratory.

"Should I be practicing with you too?" Dad asked.

India shrank away from the barrage of words. "Just being with me helps more than anything."

She was jostled out of the way by a tall boy with straggly bangs and a rather unpleasant voice. "Of course I'm going to win. Why wouldn't I? This pack of losers won't know what hit them."

"But, Marvin, you shouldn't..." His parents mumbled an apology to India and scurried after him.

There was another boy who shivered under his father's looming figure. "Of course you want to be here, son. You love spelling."

A tall, pencil-thin woman in a pantsuit and high heels was brushing a young girl's hair into two tight ponytails. "Mommy loves you. You know that. And if you win this round, I will buy you that bike you've always wanted. Wouldn't that be great?"

Nanna Flo didn't like what was going on at all. She charged up to the woman and tapped her on the shoulder. "Excuse me, but wouldn't it be great if you got on your bike instead?"

Nanna tried to look imposing, which was hard when she still had mud stuck to her clothes and face.

The woman straightened up so that she towered over Nanna Flo. "What did you say?" Her voice was steely and quiet and gave India the feeling of a wolf about to pounce.

But Nanna Flo wasn't intimidated and was about to let fly when Dad stepped between them. "She was just saying how good it would be to have a bike. To stay healthy. We could all do with more of that. Isn't that right, Nanna?"

"No, I wasn't. I—"

Luckily, at that very moment, they were interrupted by a birdlike woman onstage wearing a canary-yellow dress. She looked like she was about to burst into song. "Ladies and gentlemen," she chirped. "I am Ms. Posey, today's pronouncer. Please take your seats. We are about to begin."

Parents scrambled, some giving final hugs and advice, others pointing fingers and delivering stern warnings.

"How do you feel?" Dad asked.

India's stomach plummeted at the idea of her family having to sit far from her. "Good," she fibbed.

"Have you got your lucky hanky?" Nanna Flo asked.

India pulled it from her pocket. "Right here."

"Not that you need it," Nanna said. "You're as smart as a whip."

"Good-luck hug?" Boo held out his arms.

"Yes, please."

As Boo squeezed her tight, he whispered, "You'll be great, sis. I know it."

The Wimples moved into the audience while India took her place beside the other kids. The boy with the straggly bangs sat beside her. He flicked his hair aside, sniffed, and wrinkled his nose at India. "Did you forget to have a shower this morning?"

A few of the kids overheard and began elbowing others down the line until everyone was staring.

"I did have one, but our van broke down and..."

The boy sniffed again and scooted his chair away.

India's skin felt like it was on fire, creeping up from her toes and into her cheeks.

Ms. Posey explained the rules, but India heard none of them. Instead, she tried to discreetly pick off the mud that stuck to her clothes. But this only seemed to make things worse. Her throat tightened, her breathing grew quicker.

And the voice inside her head came back. *You're a mess. You should leave. How did you ever think you belonged here?*

India snuck a peek at the kids beside her. *They should be here—not smelly, muddy you.*

India looked into the crowd, desperately trying to find her family. She searched each row frantically. Finally, she saw their beaming faces. Dad gave a small wave, and with that, something jolted inside her. He looked so proud and happy to have his daughter onstage. India sat taller and waved back. She ignored the boy with the straggly bangs as well as the voice in her head and decided she was staying right where she was.

Ms. Posey turned to the contestants. "At this very moment, children like you, from all over the country, are hoping to win this next round and become one of the top eight to go through to the finals."

"Which will be me," the boy beside India boasted.

"So let's find out who those lucky children will be!"

One by one, each child was called. Some stumbled to the microphone; others skipped. Words were pronounced and definitions read, and after Ms. Posey judged each spelling, there were shouts and yelps, but also tears and tantrums.

Pesky.

Vexatious.

Troublesome.

Marvin, the young boy sitting beside India, was next. He swaggered across the stage, gripped the microphone, and said, "Ready when you are."

"Your word is *presumptuous*," Ms. Posey said. "This is an adjective meaning overconfident, arrogant, or cocky."

India immediately spelled it in her head.

Marvin paused and smiled a gleaming pop-star smile, confident that he knew the word but also enjoying the attention of being onstage. "Could I have the language of origin please?" he asked, drawing out his time in the spotlight.

"Middle English, old French, and late Latin."

"Thank you." He flicked his bangs and began.

"Presumptuous. P-r-e-s-u-m-t-u-o-u-s. Presumptuous."

He smiled into the cameras and waited for the applause.

"Oh dear," Ms. Posey said. "I'm afraid that is...incorrect."

Marvin's smile nosedived. "*What?*"

"Your answer is not right."

Marvin didn't budge. "It has to be right."

Ms. Posey shook her head. "I'm sorry, but it isn't, and you're going to have to leave the stage."

When Marvin crossed his arms and refused to move, Ms. Posey searched the audience. "Are Marvin's mom and dad here?"

His parents climbed sheepishly onto the stage and muttered a few words to their son, who clung to the microphone stand and cried out, "No! I demand another word!"

His dad laughed nervously. "We need to leave now, son."

"But it's not fair," Marvin wailed. "I'm better than all these other losers."

There were gasps from the audience. Marvin's parents had no choice but to pry his fingers from the stand and carry him from the stage.

He tried to pull himself from their grasp. "Let me go! There's been a mistake!"

They dragged him down the aisle to the exit, where he gripped the doorframe and kept yelling until two security guards helped his parents haul him out of the room.

"I should have been the winner!" His voice faded as the doors slammed behind him.

There was an awkward silence before Ms. Posey regained

her composure, and with a renewed smile she called the next contestant.

"India Wimple."

India's legs trembled. She carefully stood, hoping they wouldn't buckle, and tiptoed slowly to the microphone.

The voice inside her head sounded loud and clear. *Marvin thought he could win and was thrown out on his first word, so what*

chance do you have? What makes you think a mud-caked girl from Yungabilla could even think of winning?

India headed to the microphone, and with each step she felt completely and utterly...

"*Inconsequential.*"

India wasn't sure if it was Ms. Posey who had spoken or the voice in her head until Ms. Posey continued: "This is an adjective meaning of little or no importance; insignificant."

India sighed. It was exactly how she felt. She wished she could just disappear.

"India?" Ms. Posey asked. "Would you like me to repeat the word?"

"No thank you." India scribbled on her hand. "Inconsequential," she began. "I-n-c-..."

She scribbled again.

"o-n-s-e-q-u-e-n-t-i-a-l. Inconsequential."

"That is..." Ms. Posey looked up from her notes. "Correct."

India heard her family cheer wildly from the back of the room as the voice followed her all the way back to her chair. *Next time you might not be so lucky.*

The next boy looked as if he'd been dropped from a plane without a parachute. India recognized him from the lobby. He was the one whose father loomed over him. When he was given his word, he stared directly into the audience, wide eyed and frozen.

Which is exactly when the pronouncer noticed something unusual.

A man in the third row was silently mouthing the letters.

Ms. Posey nodded at the two security guards, who quickly swooped in and escorted the man away.

"What are you doing?" The man's words rang with indignation. "I've done nothing wrong! Unhand me! My son is destined for greatness!"

The boy ran after his father. "Dad!"

When they were gone, the competition continued.

Skulduggery.

Charlatan.

Manipulator.

Each time it was India's turn, she would write the word on her palm before carefully spelling it.

Industrious.

Steadfast.

Dedicated.

India peeked at the sprinkling of children remaining: only nine left. They were all staring at Ms. Posey, listening to the final words that would decide the top eight—all of them except for an Indian boy at the end of the row, who was staring at India and smiling, as if they knew each other.

Then he waved.

India panicked. She thought about waving back, but what if he was waving to someone behind her? What if he thought she was someone he knew when she wasn't? Or at least she thought she wasn't—maybe they *did* know each other but she'd forgotten.

She turned away and hoped he'd think she hadn't seen him.

The air was charged with tension. Kids spelled the final words as carefully as they could, knowing one slip could send them home.

A young girl took her place at the microphone. She nervously twirled the end of her braid, waiting for Ms. Posey to begin.

"Your word, Lily, is *outrageous*."

India instantly spelled it in her head.

The audience waited, holding its breath. No one made a sound.

Lily began. "O-u-t..." She took a deep breath. "...r-a-g..." She paused before deciding on the last few letters: "...o-u-s." She looked up hopefully.

"Oh no," India whispered.

"That is..." Ms. Posey said, "incorrect."

The audience gasped.

"You have spelled brilliantly, but sadly, it's time to say goodbye."

Lily's lip quivered momentarily. She whispered a small thank-you and left the stage.

Ms. Posey invited the eight remaining kids to stand up.

"Ladies and gentlemen, will you please congratulate our spelling bee finalists."

The audience rose to their feet and applauded, except for some not-so-polite parents of kids who hadn't won, who were busy crying or mumbling how the competition must have been rigged.

"You have all competed valiantly and made it through to the finals." Ms. Posey paused, saving the best part till last—the part India never thought she'd hear. "Which means you will all be traveling to Sydney!"

The audience cheered and lights flashed.

India felt a wave of excitement followed quickly by a wave of wanting to be sick. Her legs felt weak again, and she was about to fall over when Dad rushed onto the stage and lifted her into a hug. "You did it."

Boo squeezed between them. "I knew you would."

"Never doubted it for a second," Nanna Flo added.

"Me too," Mom agreed as they all bundled together in one giant Wimple-family hug.

The boy who smiled at her earlier was also being smothered in kisses and hugs from his mom and dad. "My son! My wonderful son!" his father repeated over and over.

Between the chaos of hugs and kisses, India noticed the boy was smiling at her. Again.

This time she smiled back—or at least tried to. She was worried it came out more like a snarl. She really had to practice, but she didn't worry about it for long because Dad interrupted with a proud declaration: "My little girl is going to Sydney."

Even as Dad announced it, he and India weren't sure they believed it—until he said with more conviction: "The Wimples are going to Sydney!"

12

SURREPTITIOUS

(adjective):

Secretive, sly, a little sneaky.

The intruder entered the yard with a surreptitious step.

INDIA'S LIFE BECAME A WHIRLWIND of school and spelling. She even dreamed words in her sleep.

Pronunciation.

Alliteration.

Orthography.

"India."

Then she started hearing Dad's voice in her sleep.

"India."

It felt real, as if he was there, whispering her name.

"India."

She opened her eyes, realizing it really was her dad's voice, and it was coming from down the hall.

She snuck out of bed and tiptoed to her parents' bedroom door, which was open just a crack.

"We owe it to India," Dad said.

"We'll think of something," Mom whispered. "We always do."

"It's a lot of money," Dad whispered back.

"Maybe we don't all need to go."

"We have to!" For a second, Dad forgot to whisper. "I promised India that the whole family would be with her."

There was a long pause before he said, "I went to the bank today to see if they'd give me a loan, but they turned me down. The manager said I didn't earn enough and the bank thought it'd be too risky. I could have lied and told him I had a few big jobs coming up, but I couldn't bring myself to do it. Are you disappointed in me?"

"Why would you say that?"

"Because I'm a journalist who unblocks toilets and clears leaves from gutters, and even then I sometimes get paid in homemade jam or hand-knitted sweaters."

"Arnold Wimple." Mom sounded angry now. India moved closer. "I never married you because I thought we'd be wealthy. I married you because you are the kindest, most considerate man I have ever met. Not only that, but you are also the handiest. If I'd known that, I would have married you sooner."

"I want to give you so much more." Dad's voice was small. "A bigger house, new clothes...a vacation every now and then."

"Why would I want all that? As long as I have you, the kids, and Nanna Flo, I have everything I need."

India crept back to her room and snuck into bed.

Over the last few weeks, she'd felt herself become less frightened when she met people she didn't know. The sick feeling she had whenever she felt nervous also seemed to disappear, which she only realized now because that sick feeling was back.

Dad felt awful—less than a dad—and it was all her fault.

India wished she'd never entered the Stupendously Spectacular Spelling Bee—then Dad wouldn't be worrying, and she wouldn't be awake worrying about Dad worrying. She wished she could go back to Friday nights in front of the TV, silently mouthing the answers, with Boo beside her and Dad, Mom, and Nanna Flo on the couch, not worrying about a thing.

India lay awake, wondering what to do. There must be some way she could help out. She tried to think about what Ingenious India would do. She was always able to get out of trouble with her brilliant plans and exceptional thinking.

Yes, but you're nothing like her. The voice inside her head was back. *She's way more daring and clever than you'll ever be.*

India sighed. *It's true,* she thought. *I'm not Ingenious India, who fights felons and fends off foes. I'm just plain old India Wimple.*

She curled into a ball and rolled toward the window.

Which was when she noticed something peculiar. Silhouetted against the streetlights, a hunched figure tiptoed silently through the night.

Directly in front of her window!

India clenched her teeth—she was furious.

Dad worked too hard for what little they had for someone to walk into their yard and steal from them. If it was a robber, she was going to let him know what a big mistake he'd made to pick their home.

She threw off her blankets and scooped up the heavy dictionary from her bedside table. She crept along the hall and into the living room, careful not to wake Boo. She slowly turned the handle of the door and gently pulled it open.

There he was!

The robber.

Sitting on their front steps.

He was crouched over and looked like he was counting something—money he'd stolen from the Wimples, probably.

India lifted the dictionary high above her head, and just as she was about to bring it down, a car drove down the street, its headlights spilling over the robber, clearly revealing his face.

"*Dad?*"

Dad turned to see India holding the dictionary. "India?"

"What are you doing here?" she asked.

"Hoping not to be clobbered by that book."

The car passed by and left them both in the dim glow of the streetlight.

"Oh." She lowered the dictionary. "Sorry. I thought you were a robber."

"They'd be out of luck if they tried to rob us." Dad laughed, but there was such a note of sadness in it that India wanted to clobber something, anything.

She sat beside him and noticed that it wasn't money he was holding but small pieces of paper. "What are they?"

Dad's worry crease deepened. "They're IOUs from jobs I've done."

"People have been paying in IOUs?"

"Not everyone, and it's only while the town's having a rough time. They'll pay me when things pick up." He brightened. "I'll find a way to pay for everything. Don't you worry."

India knew there was no other way, and it wasn't fair that her family had to find money for a competition she might not even win. So she said the only thing she could think of.

"I want to drop out of the spelling bee."

"*What?*" Dad straightened. "I'll find the money, I promise."

"It's not the money." India looked away, trying to hide the lie. "I think the stress of the competition might not be good for me. It might even be causing permanent psychological damage."

Dad raised an eyebrow. "Permanent psychological damage?"

The way he said it made it seem a little ridiculous.

"Yes." India tried to sound convincing. "Who knows how I might be affected when I'm older?"

Dad fixed her with the look of a detective. "Do you really want to drop out?"

"Yes?"

Like Dad, India was a terrible liar. And Dad knew it.

"When you were onstage, spelling all those words, did you

enjoy yourself?" India shook her head and was about to say no when he asked, "Just a little?"

India slumped. "Yes, but it's not fair to spend money on this."

"What else are we going to spend it on?"

India scowled. "How about food or the bills on the fridge?"

"And miss this chance? Not on your life." Dad pulled her closer. "We'll manage, I promise, and don't you worry about anything. That's my job as your dad."

India nestled into his hug. Moths flapped in the glimmer of the streetlight.

"Have I ever told you how we gave you your name?" Dad asked.

"About a million times." India smiled. "But tell me again."

"After college, I bought a backpack and went to India, hoping to find something incredible. And I did—I met your mom on a beach in Goa. She was the most beautiful woman in the most beautiful place. And when we got married, we wanted to name our first child after the country that brought us together."

Dad held her closer. "I'll take you there one day and show you where the Wimple family began." His smile faded and the worry crease returned. "I won't let you down, India."

"But you've never let me down. Not even close. If there were a best dad competition, you'd win it."

"Except for keeping you up way past your bedtime."

She shrugged. "No one's perfect."

Dad laughed and gave her one last squeeze. "Let's get you into bed."

Dad and India tiptoed down the hall as quietly as they could. After Dad kissed her good night and went back to his room, Boo appeared at his sister's door. India pulled back the blankets and he snuck in beside her, keeping his voice low. "Is it money again?"

India nodded. "He's worried he's let me down."

"He's never let us down. Not even close."

"That's what I told him. It's always Dad who has to fix things, but I think it's time Ingenious India stepped in."

"You have a plan?"

"Yes, but I'm going to need help to make it happen." India scrambled out of bed and put her jacket over her pajamas.

"Where are you going?"

"There's someone I have to visit."

"Not without me you're not."

India shook her head. "No way. It's cold outside. It won't be good for your... You might have another..." India couldn't say it. It always scared her when she thought of Boo having another flare-up.

Boo wasn't budging. "Ingenious India never goes anywhere without Brave Boo."

"But you can't—"

"Please, India." His voice softened. "I know you all mean well, but I'm a kid with asthma who is homeschooled and spends most of his time looking out the window at other kids having fun. Please let me come with you."

India couldn't refuse Boo's pleading eyes. "All right, but on one condition." She rifled through her closet and pulled out her warmest jacket, a wool scarf, and a beanie. "You have to wear these."

"All of them?"

India nodded. "Yes, or the deal's off."

Boo dressed quickly. The jacket hung from him like a sack. "Ready for action."

India melted a little at Boo's broad grin. "I know we all might be a little...overprotective sometimes...but as your older sister, it's my job to order you around. That's what older sisters are supposed to do. OK?"

"OK."

"Now grab your inhaler. We have a cunning plan to carry out."

~

"Mailman!"

The call came from the Wimples' front door a few days later as Dad sat glumly at the breakfast table. Ordinarily, he'd be out of bed early and in the shower, singing at the top of his off-key voice, but this morning he hadn't showered or even changed out of his pajamas. He jabbed his spoon at his porridge.

"Mailman!" This time it was shouted even louder.

Dad slumped farther into the table, wanting the world to go away.

Then the knocking started. Dad pushed back his chair and dragged himself to his feet. He opened the door to see Daryl wearing his mailman uniform and holding a large sack.

"Morning there, Arnie. Got a delivery for you."

"What's going on?" India appeared behind Dad.

"Hi, Daryl. What are you doing here?" asked Dad.

"I've got a surprise."

Boo wiggled between them. "What's going on?"

"Daryl has a surprise," India said.

"What is it?"

"We're not sure yet."

"Not sure about what?" Nanna Flo stuck her head over Dad's shoulder.

"What Daryl's come to tell us."

"What's all the noise?" Mom squeezed in beside Dad. "Hi, Daryl. What are you doing here?"

"He's come to tell us something," India said.

"Well, why don't you just get on with it, Daryl?" Nanna Flo said. "We can't stand around here all day."

Daryl sighed and handed the bulging bag to Dad.

"This is for you."

Dad peeked inside. It was filled with dollar bills and coins.

"What is it?"

"Money to get you to Sydney."

"But...*how*?" Dad asked.

"On my mail route. I asked everyone if they'd like to donate to the Wimple Family Spelling Bee Fund, and they were only too happy. And not just the people who owe you money, but those who want to see India become Yungabilla's very own champion speller as well."

India could tell Dad was overwhelmed because he bit his lip, trying not to blubber. "Thank you, Daryl," he said.

"Don't thank me—it was India and Boo's ingenious idea."

"It was?"

"They figured you do so much for this town that everyone would want to help you out."

Dad looked at India and Boo, his eyes glassy with tears. "I...I..."

"Have the best kids?" Daryl finished his sentence. "I think so too."

"You're a good egg, Daryl," Nanna Flo chimed in. "Have

been ever since you were a boy." She gave him a noisy kiss on the cheek.

He blushed. "Thanks, Mrs. W."

And, in that very moment, the Wimple family's worries of not making it to the final disappeared.

13

MAGNIFICENT

(adjective):

Impressive, majestic, very, very awesome.

Their arrival was, in every way, magnificent.

THE WIMPLES SCURRIED THROUGH THE house, packing and repacking bags. When the last piece of luggage was loaded into the van, Dad had what India thought was a very silly grin on his face—the one he wore when he was planning something sneaky.

"What's going on?" India asked.

"Nothing." Dad's smile grew wider, which only made India even more suspicious.

When they got to the town's main street, India found her answer.

People had lined up on either side, clapping and waving posters. A banner hung from one side of the street to the other:

India Wimple, Yungabilla's Champion

"They're here for you." Boo wore a smile that was even wider than Dad's.

"Nothing short of what you deserve," Nanna Flo added, wiping away a tear.

The school band was there too, and even though it was hard to tell what tune they were playing, it was very sweet.

"Did you organize this?" India asked Dad.

"It was Daryl's idea," he said, "but we helped out."

The crowd burst into raucous applause as the van drove slowly past.

"Go, India!" People waved and gave her thumbs-ups.

It was as if the whole town had come out to say goodbye—Mrs. Wild, Mrs. O'Donnell, and the entire school.

"I think they'd like a wave back," Mom said.

India was still a little stunned as she raised her hand. This made the crowd cheer and wave even more frantically.

At the end of the street, Dad pulled to a stop in front of a line of Cub Scouts headed by Daryl.

India jumped out of the van and threw her arms around him. "Thank you!"

"You're very welcome," Daryl said. "You've given the town a real boost. When you spell those words, we'll be here cheering for you."

India climbed back into the van and waved out the window as the town of Yungabilla, and everyone in it, grew smaller and smaller.

This is it, India thought. *It's really happening. We're going to Sydney.*

~~~

The drive was long, with lots of rest stops, map checking, and a picnic lunch by the river. Mom told stories, Dad led sing-alongs, and they each took turns practicing spelling with India. They tried the hardest words they could think of, but no one could stump her.

When they reached the outskirts of Sydney, the houses grew smaller and were jammed tightly together. Trucks and cars sped by in a terrible hurry. Closer to the city center, apartment and office buildings blocked the sky, and traffic crawled along the roads.

India had never seen such a flurry of activity in one place: people rushing by in business suits or on bikes, street singers, shoppers, school groups—even a man in a long, white robe, holding up a sign that said, "The End is Near."

"It'd better not be," Nanna Flo said, "or at least not until this spelling bee is over."

When they caught their first glimpse of Sydney Harbor, the Wimples fell silent. Yachts and ferries zigzagged across the sparkling water. As they drove beneath the metal arches of the
~~~

Harbor Bridge, they all craned their necks to see the white sails of the Sydney Opera House, gleaming against a perfect, blue sky.

The Wimples were amazed that they, a humble family from Yungabilla, were here in Sydney.

"We made it," Dad said, blinking away a tear.

Mom directed him through the bustling streets to their hotel. After only a few turns, she looked up from her map and pointed ahead. "This is it!"

The Wimple family simply stared.

"*This* is where we're staying?" India asked.

Mom double-checked the address. "That's what it says here."

"But it's so… so…"

"Magnificent," Boo finished.

Dad turned into the driveway and pulled up in front of the polished gold-and-glass doors of the hotel. The van backfired and lurched forward before it came to a shuddering stop.

People all around flinched.

A man in a burgundy suit and white gloves stepped over to open Nanna Flo's door, but it wouldn't budge. He tried again, this time with both hands, yanking it as hard as he could. When that didn't work, he put his foot against the van and tugged again. The handle snapped off and he almost toppled to the ground as the door creaked open. He straightened himself up and announced with a small bow, "Welcome to the Hotel Grand."

The Wimples scrambled out, and two more men in suits took their bags.

"I could get used to this," Nanna Flo said.

"Sorry about that." Dad took the handle and threw it in the back seat.

A sleek, black limousine pulled up behind them and more hotel staff moved quickly to open the doors. A young boy climbed out—the same boy who'd smiled at India during the last round.

India moved behind Dad and tried to look as small as she could.

The boy was followed by a man in a crisp, white shirt snugly stretched across a generous belly. He held a very large book and was reading out words for the boy to spell.

Which the boy was doing perfectly, India noticed.

The man was about to call out another when a small woman in a bright-blue sari stepped between them. "Let Rajish have five minutes without those blessed words."

"If he doesn't practice, how is he going to win?"

"You have been practicing for three months straight—morning, noon, and long into the night. It's time to let the boy relax."

"Relax?" The man looked as if he'd been asked to wrestle a crocodile. "We haven't come this far to risk losing now." He held a spindly finger in the air. "I am only speaking the truth."

Rajish met India's eyes. This time she didn't look away but gave him a small wave. He smiled and entered the hotel, dragging his heels after his arguing parents.

"Someone needs to lighten up," Nanna Flo mumbled.

Dad stepped in front of the hotel doors and waited for his family to gather by his side. "Ready, Wimples?"

"Ready!"

They entered the lobby, which sparkled with gold trimmings and lights that dangled from the ceiling like stars. In the center was a fountain, and on either side were opulent sofas where people in fine clothes sat sipping tea and listening to a man in a tuxedo playing a grand piano.

Nanna Flo raised an eyebrow. "If I'd known it was going to be this posh, I'd have worn my good hat." She noticed bowls of fruit sitting on tables. "Do you think these are free?"

"I'd say so," Dad answered. Before they could stop her, Nanna Flo poured the entire bowl into her bag. "And I should have brought a bigger bag."

More hotel staff hurried past carrying luggage, while others in white aprons wheeled carts layered with cream-filled cakes.

Guests mingled in excited groups, while above them a flashing sign read:

The Hotel Grand welcomes contestants for the Stupendously Spectacular Spelling Bee

Seeing it made India feel light-headed.

And slightly sick.

Dad slipped his hand into hers. "That's for you," he said.

Hearing his voice instantly settled India, as if she were a balloon he'd caught just before it floated away.

"Whatever happens from here on, you're already my champion."

Dad grabbed Boo's hand, held his head high, and put on a posh voice. "Would sir and madam like to check in?"

Boo and India followed Dad's lead and stuck their noses in the air too.

"Sir and madam would like that very much," India said.

14

IMPERIOUS

(adjective):

Overbearing, haughty, and downright bossy.

From the day she was born, she was an imperious child.

THE WIMPLES STRODE TO THE reception desk, where a man with impeccably combed hair and a perfectly pressed burgundy suit greeted them with a broad, inviting smile. "Welcome to the Hotel Grand. My name is—"

But they never heard his name, because a rather pushy girl with blond hair and a sparkly, silver coat entered the hotel, speaking in a loud, commanding voice.

"But I told you I *needed* it!" She was so loud that everyone momentarily stopped, even the piano player. The only one who didn't stop was the rather pushy girl, who marched on, while a woman scurried behind her loaded down with boxes and bags.

"Did you at least remember to pack my dress, the lace one by Dior that Mommy bought for me in New York?"

"Yes." The woman's voice rose from behind the boxes.

"And did you pack my favorite blue Armani trench coat that Daddy sent from Milan?"

She struggled to keep up. "Yes, I—"

"And have you told the organizers I only eat organic food?"

"Yes, they—"

By now she was at the reception desk. She pushed India's dad aside and rang the bell, even though, as she no doubt knew, ringing the bell was only necessary if the counter was unattended—and this one was most definitely attended.

"My name is Summer Millicent Ernestine Beauregard-Champion. I'm one of the contestants for the Stupendously Spectacular Spelling Bee."

"Let me help you," Dad said to the woman carrying the boxes, but Summer spun around as if she were about to be robbed.

"I think not! I can't have just *anyone* carrying my things. They're very expensive." Summer turned back to the receptionist. "I will not be accommodated in the standard rooms. My father has reserved the penthouse suite for me, the one with views overlooking the harbor."

She was still speaking in her overly loud voice to make sure everyone in the lobby—and even some people outside the hotel—could hear.

"Yes, madam," the receptionist said with a sour-lemon smile. "I am quite familiar with that room, but I am in the middle of serving—"

"Oh no." Dad waved his hand. "Don't worry about us. We can wait."

"They certainly can," Summer agreed wholeheartedly. "I need to go to my room immediately. It was a very turbulent flight and I'm feeling quite fraught. Oh, and my nanny will be accompanying me."

"How lucky for her," Nanna Flo muttered, which made Boo and India giggle.

Summer turned to them. "Is something funny?"

"No," Boo said. "I have this condition where I giggle when I'm excited. This, unfortunately, makes my sister giggle too."

Dad and Mom giggled into their hands. Summer shot them a glare.

"And sometimes my parents," Boo added.

Summer stepped away, worried she might catch the same giggling condition, and turned back to the desk. "Have you located my room key?"

"Here it is." The receptionist handed it over. "There will be a meeting this afternoon at two o'clock in the Grand Ballroom for all spelling bee contestants, where you'll be informed of everything you need to know for the next few days."

"My nanny, Francesca, will need to be there."

The woman carrying the boxes spoke up. "It's Daniela."

"Oh, that's right. Francesca was the last one."

Nanna Flo frowned. The more this girl spoke, the more Nanna Flo wished she'd packed her earmuffs.

"I'm afraid the meeting is only for the spellers," the receptionist explained. "Enjoy your stay." Even though he was smiling, his tone sounded more like he was suggesting she step into a pit of slimy slugs.

Summer took the key without a word of thanks and turned on her heel. Her nanny scurried quickly behind her.

Nanna Flo scowled. "Best we stay away from that one in case we catch a dose of stuck-uppity."

"That's not a word," India said.

"Yes, but it's a whole lot nicer than what I was going to say."

"Now, where was I?" the receptionist said. "Oh yes, welcome to the Hotel Grand. My name is Byron, how may I help you?"

"We are the Wimples," Dad said, "and this is my daughter, India, one of the spelling bee finalists."

"Pleased to meet you, Byron," India said.

The receptionist shook her hand. "And you too. If only everyone I met could be as pleasant as you." He sent a sharp look toward Summer, who was marching ahead while Daniela continued to struggle with the luggage. "Have you stayed at the Hotel Grand before?"

India shook her head. "We've never stayed at *any* hotel before."

"Well, young lady," Byron declared, "you are in for a real treat because the Grand is one of Sydney's finest."

He tapped the keyboard, searching for their reservation, when he noticed something else. "You know," he said in a hushed, secretive voice, "it looks as if the Grand Plaza suite is available. It has views equally as good as the penthouse."

Dad's face flushed, and he whispered, "I'm afraid, Byron, we wouldn't be able to afford—"

"There's no need to worry about that. There was a last-minute cancellation; the room has already been paid for. It would be a shame for it to go to waste."

Dad was clearly uncomfortable. "Yes, but we were told all contestants' rooms would be covered, but that families had to pay for their own."

Byron simply smiled. "Ah, but Mr. Wimple, the beauty of this room is that India and her entire family would fit very comfortably indeed. In fact, it's not so much a *room* as a glorious apartment. And it won't cost you a cent extra."

"Are you sure?" Dad asked.

"Not only am I sure, it would give me great pleasure." Byron handed over their room key. "I wish you all a pleasant stay and you, India, the very best of luck making the grand final at the opera house." He looked wistful. "Truly one of the world's most marvelous buildings. My cousin has worked there for years and says he never gets sick of it. Now, take the elevator to the penthouse floor and I will have your bags delivered to your room."

He gestured to a bellboy, who quickly wheeled over a cart and began loading their bags.

"We can carry them," Dad objected.

"It's all part of the service," the bellboy replied and whisked the cart away.

As they approached the elevators, they found Summer still barking orders at her nanny. "But I told you I wanted *pink* sheets. What do you mean they don't have any? You simply must get some."

Daniela sighed, as if she hadn't had a good night's sleep in days, maybe even weeks.

The *ping* of the elevator sounded and the doors opened. Summer bounded through first, without a thought of helping her nanny. Dad stepped forward and held open the doors.

"Thank you," Daniela mumbled from behind the boxes.

But when the Wimples went to step inside, Summer quickly

pressed the Close button. "Sorry, this elevator is fully occupied. You'll have to take the next one."

And, even though there was plenty of room, the doors closed in the Wimples' faces.

"Uppity," Nanna Flo scowled. "A word meaning arrogant, snobbish, and an enormous pain in my rear end."

Boo and India giggled.

Mom and Dad felt they should disagree—it would be the polite thing to do—but instead they giggled too and neither of them said a thing.

15

PANORAMIC

(adjective):

Extensive, scenic, a commanding view.

It was a panoramic view of the city that none of them had ever seen before.

WHEN DAD OPENED THE DOOR to the Grand Plaza suite, he was sure that they had the wrong place.

"Is this really for us?"

It was like nothing they'd ever seen and *definitely* like nowhere they'd ever been.

"I'd say so," Mom answered as they all carefully stepped into the suite, clustered together like penguins in a snowstorm. It was almost as big as their entire home in Yungabilla. There were four bedrooms with king-size beds, a kitchen stocked with food, and a spa tub the size of a small pool.

Boo stood in front of a huge TV screen on the wall. "I'm worried that if I take another step, I'll wake up."

On the table was a bowl of lollipops. This time Nanna Flo

didn't even ask before she dropped a handful of them into her bag. "In case we get hungry later."

When Dad opened the curtains, the Wimples once again found themselves staring in awe, unable to move or speak. Sydney Harbor spread out before them under a cloudless sky. For a moment, India wondered if the view was a giant painting.

Dad slid the balcony door open and the Wimples stepped outside and stood in the breeze.

"It's like being on top of the world," Boo said.

And it was. For the Wimples at least. They'd never been anywhere so high or so grand.

Dad pointed out all the famous landmarks. "There's the Harbor Bridge and the Royal Botanic Gardens and—"

"Luna Park!" Boo pointed at the famous laughing clown face that looked as if it were smiling just for them.

"Thank you, Dad," India said.

"Why are you thanking me?"

"If you hadn't convinced your friends to dress up in costumes, we wouldn't be here."

"I was just doing the time-honored fatherly duty of embarrassing myself and my friends for the sake of my kids. I'll do it again too, whenever you need me."

"Nah, I think I'm good now."

Boo coughed, his chest tight with the effort.

Mom swept to his side. "Are you feeling OK?"

"Just a little tired." He coughed again.

The Wimples knew it was more than being "just a little tired." Boo was pale and had the smallest whistling sound in his breath. It was a sound India had heard since she was a kid, and it frightened her more than any other.

"Let's get you inside, champ." Dad carried Boo back into the suite and propped him up on the couch while Mom, India, and Nanna Flo grabbed his asthma kit, pillows, and blankets.

"How's that?" India fluffed his pillows.

"Good."

She heard it again: his whistling breath. The tiniest noise that could fade away… or lead to a full-blown flare-up.

Mom pressed one puff of medication into the inhaler, and the Wimples silently counted each of his four breaths.

"Nice work." Mom spoke calmly. "You're doing well."

Dad said nothing and was almost as pale as Boo.

Boo once explained to India that asthma was like someone squeezing his chest with two large hands and sometimes, no matter how hard he tried, he couldn't make them stop.

Mom gave Boo another dose from the inhaler. He breathed in. Four breaths.

The Wimples listened and counted. One…two…three…four.

Boo's breath sounded like the wind whistling through an empty house.

This was when the Wimples' nerves would sharpen. If Boo didn't get better in the next few moments, they'd have to call an ambulance.

Another puff. Another four breaths.

India felt as if her own chest was being squeezed.

She saw Dad reach for his phone. He had emergency on speed dial.

Mom squeezed one last puff. "That's it, Boo," she said gently. "Nice, slow breaths."

One…two…three…four. Then it happened.

Boo's breathing finally became easier and the whistling faded.

"I'm OK." Boo knew only to say it when he could feel his lungs filling up again, and the Wimples' fear began to ease.

"Just as we knew you'd be." Dad slipped his phone back in his pocket.

Nanna Flo noticed the time. "India, your meeting's about to start."

India's heart was still racing from Boo's flare-up. "Maybe I'll skip it."

"Fiddlesticks! Byron said they'll have important information about the competition."

"I'd rather stay here with you."

The Wimples knew she meant *in case anything else happens to Boo*, so it was Boo who piped up next: "You have to go, so you can tell me all about it."

At times, Boo's asthma flare-ups meant there were things he missed out on—like day trips or the country fair—so the deal was, whenever this happened, India had to go and report back on everything she'd seen and done.

"OK," India reluctantly agreed, "but I won't be long."

India didn't move and Dad knew she was nervous. "Why don't I go with you?"

Nanna Flo put her hand on Dad's shoulder. "You heard Byron. The meeting is only for contestants. Plus, it will give India a chance to meet the other kids. You'll be fine on your own, won't you, dear?"

"Sure." India nodded, now even more anxious at having to leave Boo *and* mingle with strangers. Every part of her wanted to stay, but instead she said, "I'll be fine," and dragged her feet to the door.

16

DAUNTING

(adjective):

Intimidating, fearsome, even a little frightening.

It was a daunting task that left her feeling unsettled.

BUT INDIA WASN'T FINE.

That's right, she'd fibbed, but by now you know this happens with the Wimples, especially when they're trying not to hurt or disappoint anyone.

As the elevator traveled down from the top floor, her heart tripped in her chest and her breathing was shallow and fast, as if she'd just finished a race. A really long one.

When the elevator came to a stop with a *ping,* the doors opened on Rajish and his parents.

Just act normal, India warned herself.

Rajish and his mom smiled and said hello as they stepped inside.

His dad followed, his head buried in the spelling book. "Erroneous."

Rajish began spelling straightaway. "E-r-r-o-n-e-o-u-s."

"Correct. And how about—"

"Oh, leave the boy be," Rajish's mother said. "I think we've had enough for now."

Rajish gave India an apologetic shrug.

"And I think it's *wise* to keep practicing."

"Maybe being wise is overrated."

"How is being wise *ever* overrated?" his dad cried.

"When it gets in the way of what is important."

"What is *important* is our son's future, which will be brilliant if we keep practicing!" Rajish's father raised his spindly finger. "I am only speaking the truth."

The elevator came to a stop with another *ping,* and the doors opened onto the busy hotel lobby.

Rajish's parents kept arguing as all three left.

But India didn't move.

There were so many people.

Her stomach lurched as if she were hurtling down a roller coaster. She grabbed the handrail to steady herself. She was about to press the button to take her back to their room, but she couldn't. She'd made a deal.

"Come on," she said to herself. "Do it for Boo."

The Grand Ballroom was bigger than the lobby and filled with even more strangers.

There must have been hundreds of kids. They were everywhere, all milling around in groups or standing at the back of the room near tables filled with sandwiches and fruit cups.

India's chest felt tight. She wondered if this was how Boo felt when he had a flare-up. She took a deep breath, wore an extra-wide smile to hide how scared she was, and made her way to the sign-in table.

After India was given her name tag, she moved to a corner of the room and tried to pin it on her sweater, but her fingers were shaking so much she couldn't get it to work.

She tried again, this time stabbing the pin into her finger. "Ouch!" She jumped back...straight into Rajish, stomping on his toe.

"I'm so sorry," India said. "Did I hurt you?"

"Not at all." India could tell he was just being polite as he shifted from one foot to the other.

"I'm not very good at this *people* thing," she explained.

"People thing?"

"You know—talking to them, being with them."

"Which people exactly?"

"Strangers mostly." India shrugged. "Which means everyone here."

"My name's Rajish."

"I'm India."

Rajish's smile lifted right into the corners of his face. "Now we're not strangers."

"I guess not." India laughed nervously and wondered how soon she'd be able to leave.

"India—that's a nice name."

"Thank you. My parents met in India. They said it was love at first sight and promised that's what they'd name their first child."

"Very romantic," Rajish said, which made India blush even more.

"I guess. Maybe. Romantic. Sure." She knew she was babbling. *Stop talking*, she told herself.

"Are you having trouble with your name tag?"

India sighed. "I can't pin it on."

"May I?"

India froze. Not only was she now talking to strangers, but one of them was about to approach her with a sharp object.

"OK."

"I'm sorry about my parents," Rajish said, carefully pinning on the tag. "They don't normally argue; it's only since I entered the bee. My mom thought it would be kind of fun, but my dad thinks there's no point entering unless you win."

"My dad says just being here makes us champions."

"He sounds like a nice man."

"He is," India said, surprised that she was feeling more relaxed.

A shrill voice rang through the room: "Is it *organic*?"

It was Summer. Yelling at a waiter.

"I only eat *organic*." Summer's icy scowl sent the waiter scuttling away.

"That's Summer Millicent Ernestine Beauregard-Champion," Rajish said. "She flew here in her own helicopter."

"She has her own *helicopter*?" India asked.

"Sure does. Her parents are high-flying types who travel a lot, so they bought her a helicopter to help her get around when they're away. This is her first year in the spelling bee, but she completely blitzed her rounds."

"How do you know so much about her?"

"Promise not to laugh?"

India nodded.

"My father has studied all the top competitors. He says if you know your enemy, your battle is half won."

"Am *I* the enemy?" India asked.

"According to my father, anyone who stands in the way of me winning is the enemy."

India was suddenly wary. "Do you know about me too?"

"You come from a small town called Yungabilla, have a mom, dad, nanna, and brother, and this is also the first year you've competed." He smiled again, like it was the most natural thing in the world. "You blitzed your rounds too."

"Children." A voice flittered across the room. A woman with

high heels and hair twirled on top of her head like soft-serve ice cream stood before a microphone.

India's hands flew to her mouth. "Philomena Spright!"

"It's really her!" Rajish said with just as much awe.

"Congratulations on making it to the Stupendously Spectacular Spelling Bee finals. My name is Philomena Spright and I will be your pronouncer. No doubt you're all a bit nervous and, while we want you to do your best, we also want you to have fun. So, this afternoon, we've arranged a special tour of the city." There was a murmur of excited voices. "But first we'd like you to get to know each other."

"*What?*" India didn't even try to hide her horror. "She wants us to talk to each other?"

"You'll be fine," Rajish said. "You did OK with me."

"But that's because..." She tried to find the answer. "Because..."

Rajish helped her out. "Because you are naturally charming and easy to talk to."

India frowned as if Rajish had just spoken Russian.

No one—not *anyone*—had *ever* said *anything* like that to her before.

"You think so?"

"I wouldn't be standing here if I didn't."

"On your name tag is a number," Philomena Spright explained.

"Find the seat that matches that number and your new friend will be sitting opposite."

"Better go. It was nice talking to you, India Wimple."

India blushed and said, "Thanks."

In the center of the room, chairs were arranged facing each other in small circles. Kids searched excitedly for their numbered chair, but when India found hers, she quietly moaned, "Oh no."

In the chair opposite was Summer.

India sat down and attempted to smile, but even without a mirror, she knew it looked all wrong.

When everyone was seated, Philomena cheerily continued. "You have two minutes each to say your name and a little about yourself." She held up a stopwatch. "Your time starts now."

Summer crossed her arms, her whole body shouting, *I don't want to be here.*

"Would you like to start?" India asked.

"Not especially."

There was a long silence. India wasn't sure what to do next.

"Shall I start?"

"It's all so pointless." Summer scanned the room of chattering kids. "I'm here to win this spelling bee. If I'd wanted to make friends, I'd have gone to band camp."

"But Philomena said we need to—"

"Oh, all right. What's your name?"

"India."

"Interesting."

Even though Summer had said *interesting,* she didn't sound at all interested.

"My mom and dad met and fell in love in India, which was so special that they decided to name their first child India." She shrugged. "And that's me."

Summer eyed India, much like a cheetah sizing up a helpless rabbit. "So you think you're pretty *special*?"

"That's not what I meant. I just—"

"You should be careful," Summer warned. "No one likes a show-off."

"Oh, I didn't mean to show off."

Philomena rang a bell and announced, "Time to swap speakers."

India was relieved. "Your turn."

"Wimple." Summer ignored the rules of the game and stared at India's name tag. "That's an unusual name. Does it come from the root word *wimp*?"

"I don't think—"

"Alternative definitions being coward, scaredy-cat, chicken."

"I've never really thought—"

"If I were to use it in a sentence, I could say, *When I met Summer, I realized that, compared to her, I was an outclassed, hand-me-down wimp.*"

India felt as if she'd been bounced from a trampoline and crash-landed to the ground.

They sat in silence. India squirmed in her seat, not knowing who should talk next.

"Where are you from?"

"Yungabilla."

"Yunga-where?"

"It's in the country."

"So you're a hillbilly?"

"No, I—"

Philomena Spright rang the bell. "Time to make more friends! Everyone move one chair to your left."

Summer gave India a little wave. "Good luck with the competition, India *Wimp*-le."

It was obvious that Summer didn't mean it. Not one bit.

India stood up and moved to the next chair. The room went back to feeling too big, too full of strangers. She searched for Rajish but couldn't see him through the sea of kids.

India wondered how it was possible to be in the middle of a crowded room and still feel all alone.

17

FLABBERGASTING

(adjective):

Stupefying, astonishing, positively mind-blowing.

It was a flabbergasting turn of events that left them truly shocked.

"LADIES, GENTLEMEN, AND SPELLING BEE champions, welcome to your exclusive tour of Sydney," the bus driver announced. "My name is Freddie, and it will be my pleasure to show you the sights of our fair city, including a very special, *secret* destination."

Freddie's was the first in a line of open-topped, double-decker buses lined up outside the Hotel Grand.

The Wimples climbed the stairs to the top.

"How exciting." Dad sat beside Mom; he wore a red polka-dot shirt and knitted purple tie that Mrs. Butler had given him for mending her chicken coop. "I wonder what the secret destination is."

"Not sure," Nanna Flo, who was sitting next to Boo, said, "but it must be somewhere fancy, since they asked us to get dressed up."

India slid into the seat behind them.

"Are you OK back there?" Nanna Flo asked.

"Yes. Thanks, Nanna."

And it was true. Everything felt much better now she was back with her family.

Summer climbed the stairs next, wearing a willowy, blue dress with sparkling, silver shoes. She took a hanky from her matching sparkling handbag and brushed her seat before sitting down.

Her nanny staggered onto the bus, carrying a large bag. "Wouldn't you like to sit with the other children?"

Summer looked perturbed. "Why would I want to do that?"

"I just thought that maybe you'd like… Perhaps you'd enjoy…" Daniela gave up and slipped onto the seat beside her.

"Will this take long?" Summer pouted. "The flight here has left me quite worn out. I'd like to get back to my room."

Daniela looked at her notes. "A few hours, I think, but I've been told it'll be very exciting."

"I doubt that. I've seen Sydney many times before, mostly from the cockpit of Daddy's seaplane."

The nanny sank back with a resigned look that suggested she was long overdue for a vacation.

"Looks like Miss Hoity-Toity has left behind her manners again," Nanna Flo whispered to Boo and India.

Rajish's mom appeared next, wearing a rich red sari with

sparkling gold trim. India thought she looked like a princess. She smiled at the Wimples as she took the seat across from India.

Rajish's dad followed in a smart black suit and gold cravat. He was out of breath and, as usual, holding the spelling book.

"Con...ceiv...able," he puffed.

Rajish opened his mouth to spell the word, but his mom interrupted.

"Sit next to this lovely girl, son." She nodded at India, but Rajish's father objected.

"But how can I test him if we don't sit together?"

His wife smiled a very wide, knowing smile. "Precisely."

"Would you mind?" Rajish asked India.

"Not at all." India shuffled to the far edge of the seat so that she was squeezed against the side of the bus.

Rajish sat down while his parents quietly argued across from them. He couldn't help but notice how uncomfortable and squished India looked. "OK, you can say it."

"I'm sorry?" India had to make sure he was talking to her.

"You think I smell, don't you?"

"No, I don't think—"

"You can say it. I promise I won't be offended."

"No really, I—"

"Then why are you sitting so far away?"

"Oh." India edged away from the side of the bus. "I didn't want to take up too much room."

They sat in an awkward silence while everyone on the bus chatted away. India wondered how the contestants could have so much to say when they barely knew each other. Kids who'd only met hours before seemed to be best friends already.

Freddie's voice drifted over the speaker. "Now that we're all in, I want you to sit back, relax, and get ready for a day you'll never forget."

As the bus pulled away from the curb and drove through streets of stately buildings and glass skyscrapers, the laughter and excitement grew even louder. India had no idea how they did it. How everyone made friends so easily. It was like they'd all been given a friendship manual, and hers had been lost in the mail.

"We've finished the book three times now."

India hadn't expected Rajish to say anything. "Sorry?"

"The *Spelling Bee Handbook* that my dad carries with him. It has every word from every bee before this one."

"Your dad really wants you to win."

"India Wimple, you have just made the understatement of the year. Maybe the century."

India grinned. "Why is winning so important to him?"

"My father moved here from India when he was a kid. He says he was so poor that when he and his brothers weren't picking grass and weeds to thicken up their mother's curry meals, they combed through garbage dumps to find things they could sell to help the family survive."

"What about school?"

"He never went to school in India. That's why it's so important to him that I do well. He wants me to have all the opportunities he never had."

"He sounds like a good dad."

"He is." Rajish leaned closer, whispering, "But a little uptight sometimes. What's your trick to spelling words?"

"I write them on my palm with my finger to see if they look right."

"I imagine the word appearing on a screen in my head and wait until it looks like the right one."

The bus swooped around a corner and alongside the Royal Botanic Gardens, which sat perched on the edge of the harbor. India wasn't sure if it was the sun glittering on the water or the whooshing of trees that flew past, but she felt as if she were flying.

"Are you enjoying the bee so far?" Rajish asked.

Usually, India would say no to a question like that, mainly because being with strangers was never, *ever* something she enjoyed, but she realized she was enjoying herself.

"Yes," she said. "I was a little nervous during the first round, but it's been really—"

"*Irritating.*" Rajish's dad leaned across the aisle. "This is an adjective meaning infuriating or exasperating. If I used it in a sentence, I could say—"

Rajish's mom leaned across too. "Your father's obsession with winning the spelling bee is very *irritating.*"

Rajish's dad pouted. "I suppose that's one way you could use it."

His mom's hands flew into the air. "You are missing the tour."

"You are missing the bigger picture."

"You are smothering him."

"And you are holding him back. I am only speaking the truth!" Rajish's dad said, hoping to put an end to the debate.

But if the next word he chose was *seething* or *furious* or even *volcanic,* it would have perfectly described the look on Rajish's mom's face.

She grabbed the book from her husband's hands.

"What are you going to do?" he asked fearfully.

"Something I should have done weeks ago." She flung the book from the bus.

"Noooo!"

It was a flabbergasting sight.

The few people on the bus who weren't already watching finally turned around when they heard Rajish's dad cry out. The book fluttered through the air and landed on the street, where it was promptly run over by a recycling truck.

The entire bus waited to see what was going to happen next, except, that is, for Summer, who frowned and turned away from the boisterous people interfering with her tour.

Rajish's dad's nostrils flared and his eyes bulged. "Why did you do that?"

His wife took his hand. "Because, my husband, you are a *very* good man who needs to loosen up."

"But—"

"Your son is talented and smart, and he will do well because he works hard, but he also deserves to have fun."

Rajish's father softened a little. "I only want what is best for him."

"And we know that," she said.

Rajish's dad wasn't about to give up yet. "Son, what would you prefer to do: ride along on a silly tour...or practice for one of the greatest moments of your life?"

Rajish shrugged. "I'd quite like to be on the tour, Papa."

"But I thought you wanted to win."

"I do, but if it's OK, I'd rather talk with India."

Rajish's dad *and* India both looked shocked.

India's heart did one of its flips while Rajish's dad sighed. "Of course it is, son."

Rajish's mom kissed her husband's chubby cheek. "Thank you, dearest." Then she turned to India and Rajish. "Now, you two children enjoy yourselves."

And, just like that, India realized she may have made a brand-new friend, while somewhere far behind them, a recycling collector picked up a tattered book of words and threw it into the compactor of his truck, where it was squished into unreadable pulp.

18

UNEXPECTED

(adjective):

Unanticipated, unpredicted, utterly surprising.

She knew she was in for a treat, but this was most unexpected.

CAMERAS AND PHONES CLICKED AS the bus drove across Sydney Harbor Bridge.

"Not long now, folks." Freddie's voice floated through the speakers. "We're almost at our *secret* destination."

He turned off the bridge, away from the crowded lanes of traffic and into quieter, leafier streets, until they pulled up before an imposing set of iron gates guarded by men in dark suits and sunglasses.

"Welcome to Kirribilli House," Freddie announced. "The secondary official residence of the prime minister of Australia."

"Are we going to meet the prime minister?" Boo asked.

"Surely not." Nanna Flo shook her head. "He'd be too busy running the country."

"But we do have the nation's top spellers here," Rajish's dad said excitedly.

"Yes!" India's dad was getting excited too. "So he might make time for us."

The men in suits stood aside as the gates opened, and the buses trundled inside the grounds. They came to a stop before a stone building that reminded India of a doll's house. She smiled as she imagined lifting the roof and rearranging all the furniture inside.

Freddie pulled to a stop. "This is it! Your destination has been reached."

There was a feverish bustling as everyone clambered off the bus.

They were greeted by a man in an immaculate suit and perfect teeth that gleamed in the sun. "Good afternoon, and welcome to Kirribilli House. My name is Mr. Reginald Noble, and I am the house manager. Please follow me."

Dad's chest puffed out with pride. "Who would have thought the Wimple family would be invited to the home of the prime minister?"

"It is truly a great honor," Rajish's dad said with his chest equally puffed out.

As they entered the lobby, a hush settled over the group. They followed Mr. Noble across the wooden floor and under the chandeliers that sparkled like twinkling tiaras.

He flung open two doors to reveal a grand room with the longest dining table India had ever seen, decorated with candelabras and vases of bright flowers. But what was most impressive was the wall of glass doors that opened onto a lush, green lawn and a rather commanding view of Sydney Harbor and the Sydney Opera House.

Outside, waiters were putting the finishing touches on an equally long table filled with trays of sandwiches and cupcakes and, in the center, a bubbling chocolate fountain surrounded by strawberries and marshmallows.

“I could get used to this,” Dad said.

“It certainly is fancy,” Mom added.

Nanna Flo was eyeing a dish of brownies and opened her handbag, ready to sweep them in. “Do you think they would mind if I took some for later?”

Dad noticed more men in dark glasses and suits positioned around the yard, watching their every move. “Maybe it’s a good idea not to.”

Mr. Noble stood at the head of the table with a sly grin, as if he was bursting to tell a delicious secret.

“What do we do now?” Boo whispered to India.

“I guess we wait,” she whispered back.

“For what?”

“I’m not sure.”

They didn’t have to wait long, because right at that moment, two small, scruffy-haired dogs appeared from behind a bush, followed by a slightly disheveled man.

"Oh, you're here." The man's shirt was twisted, and he had a twig sticking out of his silvery hair. "Sorry I'm late." He noticed the twig and pulled it out. "I was hoping to be here when you arrived, but the terriers got a little carried away."

"Is that *him*?" India asked.

"If you mean the prime minister, then yes," Boo answered.

Two men in suits and dark sunglasses burst out of the same bushes. They brushed themselves off before taking on a serious bodyguard stance not far from the prime minister.

"Ladies and gentlemen, boys and girls," Mr. Noble announced. "May I introduce you to the official patron of the Stupendously Spectacular Spelling Bee, the prime minister of Australia?"

The crowd stood still with their mouths open, their minds frantically trying to remember everything they'd ever heard about what to do if they met the prime minister.

"Welcome to my home," the prime minister said, smoothing down his messy hair.

Still no one moved.

"Normally what happens now," he said, "is that you say some form of greeting—a simple 'Hello, Prime Minister' would be fine."

Everyone, all at once, in slightly awestruck voices, said, "Hello, Prime Minister."

"Excellent. Now that we know each other, there's no need to stand on ceremony."

One of the terriers barked. "And Sally agrees."

The prime minister continued. "As someone who loves words, I congratulate you on making it to the finals of the Stupendously Spectacular Spelling Bee. I wish you the very best of luck and, as a token of my admiration, I'd like to invite you to afternoon tea, which I always find delightful, whatever the occasion." He eyed the cakes and chocolate fountain. "With those formalities out of the way, how about we all—"

"Prime Minister." Summer pushed through the kids and parents and dipped into her very best curtsy while holding out her dress. "My name is Summer Millicent Ernestine Beauregard-Champion, and I am honored to make your acquaintance."

"Very nice to meet you, Summer. Now, everyone help yourselves—" The prime minister tried to make his way to the table, but Summer stepped in his way.

"I am a superlative speller, with exemplary results in every round."

The prime minister's eyes darted to the marshmallows sitting temptingly next to the swirling chocolate. "That's very nice."

Summer was getting frustrated that the prime minister didn't seem more impressed. "I really am possibly one of the best spellers you will ever meet."

"Which makes me very lucky." He held up his hands before Summer could say anything else. "Please, everyone, you must eat because I won't be able to finish all this on my own." He hurried to the table, swiped a marshmallow through the melted chocolate, and popped it into his mouth. "I've been dreaming about this all afternoon." He turned to the Wimples, who stood transfixed beside him.

"And what's your name?" the prime minister asked Boo.

"Boo Wimple, and this is Dad, Mom, Nanna Flo, and my sister, India."

The Wimples performed a clumsy combination of bowing and curtsying.

"Are you one of the spellers?"

"No, India is. She's one of the smartest people in Yungabilla, maybe even Australia."

"Boo." India blushed.

"It's true," Dad said.

The prime minister frowned. "Can't say I've heard of Yungabilla."

"You will soon, when India wins the grand final," Nanna Flo said before popping the rest of her cupcake into her mouth.

"Nanna." India wished her family would talk about something else.

"Sorry, India," the prime minister said, "but being part of a family means they have the right to say embarrassingly nice things about you, whether you like it or not."

"Can I ask you a question?" Boo said.

"As your prime minister, I'd say yes."

"When you came out of the bushes, was that a secret escape route?"

"Yes," the prime minister whispered conspiratorially. "I have several of them around the grounds and a tunnel beneath the property for whenever I need to make a quick escape."

"From *danger*?" Boo asked.

The prime minister picked the chicken from a sandwich and sneakily threw it to the terriers. "From danger of being *bored.* I love being prime minister, but you can meet some terribly boring adults sometimes, so that's when I sneak away."

India and Boo giggled.

"I was quite a good speller as a child," the prime minister continued. "My brother and I would lie in bed at night and have competitions. We'd find the trickiest word and see if the other one could spell it. I was so determined to win sometimes I'd fall asleep over the dictionary."

"I do that too!" India cried a little more loudly than she intended.

The two men in suits moved in fast. "Everything all right, sir?"

"Absolutely!" the prime minister said. "Couldn't be better."

The men moved away, keeping an eye on everyone.

"Now one of my favorite things to do is watch the bee in my pajamas with the family."

"We do that too." India couldn't believe a girl from Yungabilla could have so much in common with the prime minister of Australia.

"What's your favorite word?"

"*Illustrious,*" she answered without hesitation. "I like the way it sounds."

"Mine is *smorgasbord.*" The prime minister wore a mischievous grin. "I like all the cold cuts."

India had never thought of the prime minister as smiley. Every time she'd seen him on TV, it was to announce something serious, which often meant he looked as if he had a terrible toothache.

"I'd better go mingle." He picked up a cupcake with a strawberry nestled on a swirl of cream. "Good luck, India." He leaned in closer. "I'm not supposed to play favorites, but I'll be watching from home, quietly hoping you win."

India thought that this was perhaps the most exciting moment of her life so far. "Thank you, Prime Minister."

"How about that." Dad had a tear in his eye. "A prime-ministerial good luck."

"It doesn't get much better than that," Nanna Flo said, before sneaking some scones into her bag.

The Wimples huddled over the cakes and sandwiches, talking excitedly about what the prime minister had said, while only a few steps away, an infuriated young girl in a blue dress had overheard it all—making her so angry she thought she might burst.

She glared at one person in particular and whispered a vow: "The prime minister can wish you all the luck in the world, but there is no way you are going to beat me, India Wimple."

19

DISQUIETUDE

(adjective):

Anxiety, agitation, and generally feeling off-kilter.

The hectic events of the day left them with a feeling of disquietude.

INDIA LAY IN HER KING-SIZE bed at the Hotel Grand, her head bustling with thoughts: the tour through Sydney, meeting the prime minister, and the spelling bee finals tomorrow.

But there was something else.

Rajish.

I'd rather talk with India.

Of all that had happened in the last twenty-four hours, this is what she remembered the most. Not only did he sit next to her on the bus, but he was also funny and nice, and he wanted to talk to her.

And it *wasn't* awful.

She even...enjoyed it.

And she absolutely had never, ever enjoyed talking with strangers.

Until now.

She laughed, which was exactly when Mom poked her head in the room. "Something funny?"

India wasn't ready to tell her about Rajish. Instead, she told sort of a fib. "I can't get to sleep because I keep thinking about everything that's happened."

Mom sat on the bed beside her. "Are you nervous about tomorrow?"

"A little, but I think I'm OK."

Mom reached for a small package that was hidden inside her bathrobe. "I was going to give you this tomorrow, but since you're still awake, you might as well have it now."

India tore off the paper and held up a sleeveless, red dress sprinkled with small purple flowers.

"I added a pocket for Great-Grandpop's hanky."

"You made this?"

Mom nodded. "While you were at school. I thought it'd be nice to have a brand-new dress for your big moment."

"It's perfect." India hugged her mom. "Thank you."

"What's going on?" Dad was at the door.

"India can't sleep."

"What's up?" Boo appeared beside him in his rumpled robot pajamas.

"India can't sleep," Mom said.

"Is everything OK?" It was Nanna Flo this time.

"India can't sleep," the Wimples answered in unison.

"It's to be expected," Nanna Flo said.

Mom saw the dictionary beside India's bed. "Would you like us to practice with you?"

India shook her head. "Could I hear a story instead?"

"Which one would you like?"

"Brave Boo and Ingenious India."

The Wimples climbed into India's king-size bed and snuggled up as Mom began.

"There once was a girl called Ingenious India, who had a brother called Brave Boo. Together, they once saved the prime minister from a *perilous plot* of *treacherous turmoil…*"

As Mom told the story, adding in the details of tenacious terriers and top-secret subterranean tunnels, on the other side of the hotel wall, in the palatial penthouse suite, Summer was having trouble sleeping too.

Her nanny had long ago said good night, and Summer now stood at the window, with all of Sydney twinkling far below.

She watched boats sail by with party-loads of people, the Ferris wheel at Luna Park turning in the distance, cars and buses filled with passengers, all with somewhere to go.

And someone to go with.

She clambered into her enormous bed, which overflowed with stuffed toys, each one bought by her parents as a present from another business trip. She knew each one by name and liked to pretend they were her brothers and sisters.

She cuddled up beside them, holding out her phone to make sure they could all see the screen as she played videos of her and her parents at birthday parties, playing on the beach, and on a pier sharing a giant ice-cream sundae.

There weren't many, but she watched them all, over and over again.

"Would you like to speak to Mommy and Daddy before we go to sleep?" She nodded the head of a fluffy dog beside her. "OK." She wagged a finger. "But not for long. It's way past your bedtime."

Summer pressed a number into her phone and waited. Her face filled with an expectant smile. Then she heard a familiar voice: "Hello, you have reached Evelyn Elizabeth Marigold Beauregard. I am in Auckland and unable to take your call at this time, but if you leave me a message, I will phone you back at my earliest possible convenience."

Beeeeep.

"Hello, Mommy. It's Summer. I just wanted to say…to say… good night." And because she wasn't sure what else to say, she said, "So…good night."

But then she changed her mind. "Actually, there is something else. I've made it to the—"

Beeeeep. Message ended. Please call back if you would like to leave a further message.

Summer stared at the screen as it went black. She laid the phone on the bedside table, opened the drawer, and pulled out a red pencil and a small notebook. Inside the notebook was a foldout map of the world. It was filled with red dots from South Korea to Hong Kong—even as far away as Denmark. She took the pencil and added a dot beside Auckland.

She stared at the map before folding it up and placing the book back in the drawer. She sank down into her large bed filled with stuffed animals and stared at the lights of Sydney until she slowly drifted off to sleep.

20

DISAGREEABLE

(adjective):

Ill tempered, peevish, discourteous, impolite, churlish, disabling, ratty. (There are just so many words for this one.)

She was a thoroughly disagreeable child.

"HOW DO I LOOK?" DAD made a fittingly grand entrance into the living room of the Grand Plaza suite.

The Wimple family froze. Nanna Flo held a brush halfway through India's hair. Boo was in the middle of tying his shoes, and Mom stood with lipstick on half a lip.

Dad turned before them, proudly modeling a pair of yellow-and-red-striped pants.

"Mrs. Gadsby made them for me after I unclogged her sewer pipe." Dad shuddered. "That one was a nasty job," he said before pulling up the legs of his trousers. "So she threw in these green polka-dot socks."

Boo, Nanna Flo, Mom, and India stared, not sure what else to do. Finally, Mom spoke up.

"They're..." she began, but nothing else came out.

Dad's shoulders drooped. "Ridiculous, aren't they? I knew it."

"No!" Mom cried. "I love them."

"You do?"

"Of course," Mom fibbed, much to the relief of the other Wimples. "In fact, I don't think there's anyone else handsome enough to carry them off." She kissed him on the cheek. "Now, we have a spelling bee to get to."

~

The elevator opened onto a lobby crowded with nervous parents and spelling bee contestants.

"This is it," Dad said, rubbing his hands together. "The moment we've all been waiting for."

Mom gave Dad one of those looks that told him he'd gone too far. He dropped his hands. "What I meant to say is that we love you very much, India Wimple, and no matter what happens today, we're very proud of you."

"Oh pish!" Nanna said. "My money's on India taking home that trophy."

"Excuse me, everyone." They turned to see a woman wearing a microphone headset. "All spellers need to go to wardrobe to get ready for the broadcast."

This time, the entire round was going to be live on national TV.

India's heart did a flip—one of the old-fashioned ones, where she suddenly felt very anxious.

The Wimples began what had become their special routine of saying goodbye.

"Go get 'em, sweet pea." Dad gave India an extra-long hug.

"Don't forget your great-grandfather's hanky," Nanna Flo said. "Give it a quick squeeze before you start."

"I will."

"Good-luck hug?" Boo asked.

"Yes, please." Her voice wavered a little, and Boo could hear it.

"You'll be great, sis," he whispered. "I know it."

Mom gave India a final kiss on the forehead, and the Wimples waved as she headed off, but with each step India's nerves frayed.

And the voice inside her head came back: *Why did you think you could even do this?* it said. *You're not just going to freeze in front of a few hundred people like you did during the school play—you're going to freeze in front of millions.*

Then she saw Rajish.

His dad was giving him a last-minute pep talk when his eyes met hers. He smiled and gave her a sneaky wave. India waved back, and in that moment, she felt her nervousness fade.

Maybe that's all there was to friendship—there wasn't any

magic to it or a manual to tell you how it works. You just had to be with the right person.

India turned and, with a spring in her step, followed the signs to the girls' wardrobe area.

Which is where she saw Summer.

"Ah, India Wimp."

"It's Wimple." India took off her sweater.

"Oh, yes. That's right." Summer turned away and flicked through dresses dangling from a clothes stand. "Was that your family in the lobby?"

"Yes," India said proudly.

"Are they performers?"

"Sorry?"

"I thought perhaps they were performers," Summer said. "Those pants your dad is wearing are real showstoppers."

"My dad's a repairman."

"How quaint. Who's the old lady? Is she your nanny?"

"No, she's my—"

Summer turned away, not even bothering to hear the answer. "What are you wearing for the competition?"

India looked down at the red dress her mother had made. "I was going to wear this."

"Oh." It was obvious that Summer was less than impressed. "I can't decide on the trench coat by Armani or the Stella McCartney jumpsuit. My father says that when you enter a room, you should make an impression, and I want to make a big impression when I walk onto that stage."

Her face lit up. "This one." She held a flowing, white dress against her. India thought she looked like a glamorous model, with her perfectly styled blond hair. "And these will make it perfect." Summer chose a pair of strappy heels and headed off to the changing rooms.

India watched her leave, suddenly feeling incredibly small, as if she were actually shrinking.

Minuscule.

Inconsequential.

Nugatory.

The room swirled with girls in beautiful dresses huddling in groups and posing for selfies.

The voice in India's head came back. *This isn't for you. It's for rich, beautiful girls, just like you expected.*

"India Wimple?" The makeup artist held up a brush. "I'm Trudy, and it looks like you're next."

India slunk into the chair while Trudy redid her ponytail.

A group of girls behind them erupted into giggles as they leaned in to each other and whispered conspiratorially. India looked down into her lap.

"Is everything OK?" Trudy asked.

India nodded. "Just a little nervous."

"Nerves can be good. They can keep you on your toes. You'll be fine."

India tried as hard as she could to believe it.

"Ten minutes to on air!" the floor manager called. "Time to go, everyone."

India shrank behind the others as they were led backstage. Outside, she could hear the excited mutterings of the audience.

Philomena Spright was in the wings, warming up her voice. "The rain in Spain falls mainly on the plain. How now brown cow..." The light from the stage covered her in a radiant glow so that she shimmered in her gold dress, just like a movie star.

"Five minutes, everyone."

India's heart quickened. She took a deep breath, trying to slow it down.

"This is it." Rajish appeared beside her. "Our big moment. Are you ready?"

"I think so." India nodded, wanting it to be true.

"You'll be great," Rajish said. "I know it."

"Good luck, everyone," Philomena said as the audience began to settle. "And remember, enjoy yourselves."

The floor manager led the spellers to the chairs onstage.

India held her hand against the glare of the lights. She searched for her family, but apart from the people in the front row, the audience was shrouded in shadow.

Her head was a muddled jumble of letters and words—none of them made sense. India dipped her hand into her pocket and gave her great-grandfather's hanky a squeeze, and she felt a little better.

Every kid on either side of her was nervous too, judging by their fidgeting hands and jiggling knees. Every kid, that is, except Summer, who sat perfectly still, waiting for the cameras to roll.

"Have a great show, everyone." The stage manager held her fingers in front of the main camera and counted down. "We're going live in four...three...two..." Her hand dropped and the theme music started.

Philomena Spright beamed into the camera. "Welcome to the finals of the Stupendously Spectacular Spelling Bee!"

The audience erupted into applause, the music blared, and searchlights lit up the stage.

"Over the next two exhilarating rounds, we will discover who is going to be our new champion. Tonight, each speller is allowed one incorrect answer...but any more than that means we say goodbye. At the end of the night, we will have our top twelve spellers, who will go on to compete in the grand final." Philomena paused. "At the world-famous *Sydney Opera House*!"

This sent the audience into another excited round of applause.

"So, let's begin."

Children were called to the microphone and Philomena Spright carefully pronounced each word.

Enthusiastic.

Rhapsodic.

Euphoric.

India practiced writing each word on her hand, but every attempt confused her even more.

Chronicle.

Labyrinthine.

Was it *chronical* or *chronicle*? Was it *laberinthine* or *labyrinthine*? She wasn't sure which ones were right.

She searched the audience again, hoping to see Dad's wave, realizing how much she needed it, but the stage lights were so bright she couldn't see anything but an endless stretch of black.

Flummoxed, the voice in her head said, more snarky than usual. *A verb meaning to be confounded, bewildered, or completely stumped.*

"India Wimple."

"Yes?"

Philomena was staring directly at her—and may have been for quite some time. "Your turn."

Some of the audience laughed.

India stepped gingerly to the microphone.

"Your word is *infinitesimal*."

She immediately wrote it on her hand. Did she have her *i*'s and *e*'s in the right place? Did it end in *el* or *al*? Or maybe *le*? She tried it again and again, but nothing looked right.

"Fifteen seconds remaining." Philomena Spright gave her a hopeful look.

"Infinitesimal," India began. "I-n-f-i-n..." She scribbled on her hand. "i-t..."

"Time's almost up," Philomena said. "I need an answer."

Slowly, she spelled the rest of the word: "i-s-i-m-a-l."

She heard a gasp from the spellers behind her.

Philomena looked down to double-check her card. "That is… incorrect."

India felt as if a weight had landed on her chest. She nodded to the pronouncer and trudged back to her seat. She slumped forward, staring at her shoes, barely hearing the next words. *You shouldn't be here,* the voice said. *Summer was right. You're not even dressed properly.*

"Rajish Kapoor."

India watched Rajish walk to the microphone. He looked relaxed and was smiling.

"Your word is *erroneous.*"

Rajish thought about it, frowned, and thought some more.

India stared in disbelief, wondering why he hadn't begun spelling.

"Erroneous." Rajish paused again, as if he was deciding what to do. "E-r-r-o-n-i-o-u-s. Erroneous."

He looked hopefully at Philomena Spright.

"I'm afraid that's incorrect."

Rajish shook his head, and, as he made his way back to his seat, he snuck India the smallest smile.

India was confused. Rajish knew that word. She'd heard him spell it in the elevator with his dad.

More contestants came and went. More words were spelled incorrectly. Slowly the number of children was whittled down.

And the words became harder.

Kaleidoscope.

Reconnaissance.

Onerous.

India had spelled four words correctly and was feeling more comfortable when she was called back up to the microphone.

"Your word is *indefatigability*."

She needed to get this right or she would be out of the competition.

"I-n-d..."

Was it an *a* next...or an *e*? She wrote on her hand. "e-f-a-t..."

Then she saw it, as if the spelling had formed on a screen in her head, like Rajish said it would.

"i-g-a-b-i-l-i-t-y."

"That is correct!" Philomena Spright waved the card.

When India walked back to her chair, Rajish was staring at her with a look that said, *See? I told you you'd be great.*

The room was tense. The audience sat in nervous silence, hanging on every letter, waiting anxiously for each verdict.

India glanced at the empty seats onstage and the twelve kids who were left. They all had a chance at the grand final, but one of them had to go.

"*Solecism,*" Philomena announced. "This is a noun meaning a mistake or blunder."

Even though the word wasn't long, India knew it was tricky. She closed her eyes and watched it form in her head.

The boy at the microphone began. "Solecism."

India heard the doubt wavering in his voice.

"S-o-l-e…" He stopped suddenly, as if he'd changed his mind.

"Fifteen seconds." Even Philomena sounded nervous.

The boy chewed his fingernail. Time was running out. He had to make a decision. "…s-i-s-m. Solecism."

Philomena reluctantly answered, "That is…incorrect." The audience sighed all at once. "But you have spelled brilliantly and should be very proud that you are one of our country's top spellers."

She led the audience in a round of applause before the boy was ushered from the stage. "Ladies and gentlemen, we have our top twelve!"

India could hardly believe it. She looked at Philomena, who clapped enthusiastically, and then at Summer, who posed for the camera with her best polished smile. And finally at Rajish, who was looking straight at her, his face lit up like a Christmas tree.

21

SAGACIOUS

(adjective):

Clever, intelligent, and a little bit crafty.

It was a sagacious idea she hoped would work.

RAJISH RUSHED OVER TO INDIA. "We made it! We're in the grand final."

India was still having trouble believing it was true when Rajish spotted something over her shoulder and his beaming smile instantly faded away. "If we survive."

"Survive what?"

"*That.*"

India turned to see the Wimples and Kapoors rushing onto the stage. They braced themselves as their stampeding families once again smothered them in hugs and kisses.

Dad lifted India into the air. "My little champion!"

"You were most impressive, my boy," Rajish's dad gripped his shoulders. "There was the one *erroneous* mishap, of course, but—"

"We won't mention that," his mom said in a warning tone, "because we are so proud of you."

"Yes!" Rajish's dad said. "Of course we are. And now we must celebrate! Wimple family, my cousin has an Indian restaurant not far from here, and it would be our great honor if you would be our guests."

"At a real restaurant?" Boo asked.

"Not only is it real," Rajish's dad said, "it is the best Indian food outside of India. What do you say?"

"Could we, Dad?"

Dad looked uncomfortable. "I'm not sure we could accept such a generous—"

"You don't like Indian food?" Rajish's dad frowned.

"Yes, we do," Dad said.

"Do you have other plans?"

"No."

"Then it is decided." He slapped India's dad on the back. "We cannot let this momentous night pass without a celebration. How fast can you kids get ready?"

"I need to grab my sweater from the dressing room," India said. "Is five minutes too long?"

"Make it three and you have a deal." Rajish's dad rubbed his stomach. "All that tension has made me famished."

India tore through the corridors and into the girls' dressing room. She reached for her sweater and heard a voice through the racks of clothes.

"That's OK, Mom. Of course, I don't mind."

India stepped closer and peeked through the dresses. It was Summer, hunched over a table, speaking on her phone.

"I know you're both very busy." Her face creased with worry, just like India's dad's did. She listened before adding, "I love you too."

Summer took the phone from her ear and stared at it as if it were broken. "I miss you," she muttered and started to cry.

India felt bad about eavesdropping. She thought she could tiptoe away and pretend she hadn't heard.

But she couldn't. It didn't seem right.

"Summer?"

Summer startled and quickly turned her back on India. "What do you want?" She picked up a brush and jammed it through her hair.

"Are you OK?"

"Of course I'm OK." She stared into the mirror. "I am on the verge of being crowned the world's greatest speller. Why wouldn't I be OK?"

"I heard you on the phone."

Summer didn't answer.

"I'm sorry your parents aren't coming to the grand final."

She brushed even harder. "They can't just drop everything and be here. It's easy for your parents when they don't have real jobs."

It was one of the meanest things Summer had ever said, and it stung India just as she'd intended.

Summer stopped brushing her hair and, for a second, it seemed as if she might apologize...

But she didn't.

She slammed down the brush. "I need to get changed. My father has arranged for Daniela to take me to a very fancy restaurant." Summer scooped up some clothes and headed for the changing rooms.

India still smarted from the comment about her parents. She wanted to leave and get as far away from Summer as possible, but there was a small part of her that kept thinking about how sad Summer had looked when her mom said she couldn't be there.

Then India saw it. Summer's phone. Poking out of her bag.

She looked around to make sure she was alone before she picked it up and looked up the last number dialed. She quickly scribbled it down with eyeliner on a tissue before replacing the phone exactly as she found it and hurrying out of the room.

Where she bumped into Rajish.

And stepped on his toe.

"I'm sorry," she said.

"It's OK." He was obviously in pain. "But if it happens again, I'm going to take it personally. Papa sent me to ask if you're ready."

"There's one thing I need to do first. Do you have a phone I can borrow?"

"It'll have to be fast—he's convinced he's going to fade away if he doesn't eat soon."

India pressed the numbers from the tissue into Rajish's phone.

"Who are you texting?"

"Two people who need some very urgent information that may change their lives."

India typed as fast as she could:

Dear Summer's parents,

You must be very proud that your daughter is in the grand final of the Stupendously Spectacular Spelling Bee. This makes her one of the best spellers in this country, maybe even the world! I know she said she didn't mind that you couldn't make it, but she misses you both so much and would love more than anything if you could be here for her big moment. It's at the Sydney Opera House tomorrow at 5:30 p.m.

Yours in anticipation,
Summer's friend,
India Wimple

India handed back the phone. "Now, let's go save your dad from imminent demise."

~~~

Rajish's dad was in charge of ordering the meals at the restaurant, which meant there was so much food that India wondered how they'd ever finish it.
~~~

"Eat, please, eat!" He dished out huge servings of butter chicken onto mounds of saffron rice.

When he sat down, Rajish's mom planted a kiss on his cheek.

"What was that for?"

"Because you are a very good man"—Rajish's mom held up her finger—"and I am only speaking the truth." The others laughed as she gave him another kiss, this time with a loud *smack*!

India was about to dig in when Rajish whispered, "Thank you."

"For what?" she asked.

"If it hadn't been for you, my mother may never have thrown away the spelling book, I would have missed the tour of Sydney, and my parents would still be arguing. And," he added, "I wouldn't have had the chance to get to know you better, which has been the best part of the spelling bee."

At this point, the old India would have made an excuse to leave the table and escape through the nearest exit. Instead, she simply said, "That has been my favorite part too."

Rajish's smile was back, bigger than ever.

"I also saw what you wrote to Summer's parents."

"I know she hasn't been very nice, but I think it's because she misses them. I'd be grumpy too if my family couldn't be with me."

"And that, India Wimple, makes me like you even more."

India blushed, and they continued eating their butter chicken, which was as delicious as Rajish's dad had promised.

"Can I ask you something?" India lowered her voice so no one could hear. "Did you deliberately misspell your word today?"

"Why would I do that?"

"I don't know, but I heard you spell *erroneous* in the elevator."

Rajish shrugged. "I buckled under the pressure."

India scowled. "You didn't *look* under pressure."

"I hide my nerves well."

"I don't believe you."

Rajish faked being shocked. "You think I'm lying?"

"Yes." India smiled. "And that makes me like you even more."

~

In the taxi on the way back from the restaurant, the city lights twinkled around the Wimples as though they were in their very own fairy tale. The night had been perfect, but India had one more plan to carry out before it was over.

"Here we are." The taxi driver pulled to a stop.

Nanna Flo, who had been dozing in the back, woke up. She looked around. "This isn't the hotel."

"We know." India smiled. "We have to make a small pit stop first."

Nanna stepped out of the taxi and was shocked by what she saw next.

"*The Sydney Opera House*," she whispered in awe. "She's even more beautiful up close."

Its wide, arching sails glowed against the starry night.

"Come on." India offered Nanna her arm. "This way."

"Where to?"

"You'll see."

They wove through the bustling crowds and up the many stairs to the glass doors, where a security guard seemed to be waiting just for them.

"Good evening. I'm Arlo, Byron's cousin. You must be the Wimples, here for your special performance."

"We sure are," India said.

"Excellent. Follow me."

Nanna Flo turned to Dad. "What's your daughter up to?"

"You're about to find out."

After winding their way through a labyrinth of stairs and corridors, Arlo opened a door into a gigantic theater with rows of seats stretching into the distance and a vaulted, wooden ceiling high above. "Welcome to the Concert Hall of the Sydney Opera House." He looked at his watch. "I can give you ten minutes before I need to lock up. Enjoy the show."

Nanna Flo turned slowly on her heels. "It's magnificent—much more so than I ever thought it would be. What's the performance?"

The Wimples didn't answer and instead took their seats in the front row.

"You." India beamed.

"What?"

"We're here to see *you,*" Dad said, getting comfortable in his seat.

"This is your chance to sing at the Sydney Opera House," Mom said.

"Oh, I couldn't."

"Yes, you could," Boo said. "If India can overcome her nerves to join the spelling bee, you can sing."

"So you're all ganging up on me?"

"Yes, we are," India said, "but we only have eight minutes left before we have to leave. You've always wondered what it would have been like to sing at the opera house. Now here's your chance. What do you say?"

Just glancing at the stage made Nanna Flo's whole body tingle. "I suppose so. Since we're here."

India sat beside Boo as Nanna Flo made her way onto the stage. She stood in the very center, under a single spotlight. "Don't complain to me if I'm a little rusty."

Nanna closed her eyes, took a deep breath, and began to sing.

And it was beautiful. Her voice lifted into the ceiling and made the Wimples feel as if they were floating.

After the last note faded, the Wimples gave her a standing ovation. It was simply the best performance they had ever seen.

22

MOMENTOUS

(adjective):

Significant, unforgettable, earth-shatteringly huge.

It was a momentous occasion they never thought they'd experience.

IT BEGAN AS AN ORDINARY day: the sun rose; the birds chirped; people everywhere began to stretch and yawn.

But for India Wimple, this was no ordinary day.

As she lay in bed, she tucked her hands behind her head. In the last few months, she had won three rounds of the Stupendously Spectacular Spelling Bee, met the prime minister, arranged for Nanna Flo to perform at the opera house…

And she'd made a new friend.

She may even have been kind of *ingenious* in fixing the problem of Summer's *irascible, cantankerous* behavior.

But it was too early to know that yet.

"Time to get up, sweet pea." Dad was dressed in yellow pajamas blooming with giant sunflowers.

"Nice pj's," India said.

Dad paraded around in them, catwalk style. "Mr. Stevens gave them to me for rebuilding his fence when he accidentally backed his car into it." India laughed and Dad plonked on the bed beside her. "You don't like them?"

"They're perfect." India leaped into Dad's arms. "Thank you."

"What for?"

"For being my dad."

He gave her one of his extra-special Dad hugs. "I wouldn't have it any other way."

Wearing their pajamas and fluffy hotel slippers, the Wimples took turns practicing some last-minute spelling over a lavish breakfast of pancakes with strawberries and maple syrup.

Exhilaration.

Euphoria.

Exuberance.

Nanna's curlers bobbed on her head as she cheered each correct answer. "That's my girl!"

Then Dad added a doozy.

Honorificabilitudinitatibus.

"That is not a word," India objected.

"It's from Shakespeare, and it means *the state of being able to achieve honors*. Something you should prepare for when you receive your prize after winning—" Dad was stopped by Mom's scowl. "I mean, of course, win or lose, we know you'll do your best."

"Boo!" India called over her shoulder. "We need you. Dad's making up words."

"I am not."

They heard the shower from the bathroom in Boo's bedroom.

"You'd better go and get him," Dad said as he reached for another pancake, "or we're going to have to order more of these."

India knocked on the bathroom door and opened it a fraction. "Boo, you have to come quick. You're missing all the pancakes."

When he didn't answer, she pushed the door open a little wider. "Boo, Dad's eating all the—"

India froze.

Boo was on the floor, hunched over, dressed only in his pajama pants.

Gasping for air.

"Dad! Mom!" she cried. "Boo can't—"

Mom squeezed past India, lifting Boo's head, which flopped like a broken doll's.

Dad picked him up, carried him to the sofa, and sat him upright. "Hey, little fella. We're here now."

Nanna Flo rushed out of Boo's room with the inhaler and spacer.

Boo's eyes lolled open and closed.

Mom held the spacer to his mouth and pressed on the inhaler. "You have to breathe in, Boo. I know it's hard, but you have to do it."

Boo tried, but he couldn't draw enough oxygen into his body. India could see his ribs sucking in and out, as if he were trying to breathe through a straw.

It wasn't working.

"Take slow, deep breaths," Mom said. "That's it. You can do it."

India saw Mom trying to be calm, Nanna Flo rubbing Dad's back, and Boo struggling for breath. His body was being squeezed of every last scrap of air.

Dad held him upright, but his little body continued to sag. He was pale and his skin shimmered with sweat.

Mom tried the inhaler and spacer again. He struggled to take even one breath.

The medication wasn't working.

Mom was the calm one, the one everyone looked to, the one who would make sure Boo would be OK, but the worry on her face was inescapable.

Nanna Flo picked up the phone. "Ambulance. Asthma attack. Hotel Grand."

Then India saw it—the one symptom doctors had warned them about, the one they all feared the most.

Boo's lips were turning blue, and his body crumpled in Dad's arms.

23

NERVOUS

(adjective):

Fearful, uneasy, very, very scared.

It was a nervous wait that left them anxious.

INDIA STAYED BY BOO'S SIDE and held his hand even after the ambulance arrived.

"My name's Levi," one of the paramedics said to Boo as he worked quickly to fit him with an oxygen mask. He nodded toward his partner. "And he's Roy."

India watched as Levi drew medication into a syringe and attached it to the mask. "This is a Ventolin nebulizer, which will open your airways. I know things might feel a little scary, but we're taking you to the hospital to get you fixed up right away."

They carefully lifted him onto the stretcher and wheeled him into the corridor. The Wimples crammed into the elevator, each of them wishing it would go faster.

Boo's heavy eyelids drifted open and closed.

Byron was waiting for them downstairs and directed people out of the way as the paramedics flew through the lobby. He held the door open and gave India a small wave before they rushed outside.

Every time Boo had a flare-up, the Wimples were never sure how bad it would be or how long it would take him to recover, but in the backs of their minds, they worried that this would be the one that would be too much for his small body.

Levi kept talking to Boo. "Hang in there, little man. And hold on tight, because you're about to have the ride of your life."

They slid the stretcher into the ambulance. India felt Boo's hand slip away from hers. Dad and Roy squeezed in beside Boo.

India tried to climb inside, but Levi gently held her back. "Sorry, there's no room." He closed the doors and hurried to the cabin.

"I *have* to go with him," India pleaded. "He's my brother."

"I'm sorry," Levi said, climbing into the driver's seat. "We'll see you at Saint Michael's."

Mom pulled India close as the siren blared and the ambulance careened down the street.

"Don't worry, India." Byron hailed a taxi. "You'll be there just as fast. I promise."

Nanna Flo took charge after they scrambled inside the cab. "Saint Michael's Hospital," she told the driver. "I'll give you an extra fifty bucks if you can keep up with that ambulance."

The taxi driver smiled. "I'll do better than that."

They swerved through the city streets, following the ambulance with its wailing siren and flashing lights. Cars stopped and pulled out of their way, but each second India was away from Boo felt too long.

"Do you think he'll be OK?" she asked Mom.

Mom would always hold India close at times like this and answer, "Of course he will. You wait and see." But this time, when Mom began to speak, her voice cracked, like the words were stuck in her throat.

It was Nanna Flo who said what they all wanted to hear. "Of course he will. He's a Wimple, and we Wimples never give up. He's going to be just fine."

When the hospital finally appeared, the taxi came to a screeching stop out front, just as the ambulance turned into the entrance. Nanna opened her purse and handed the driver his money.

"Keep it," he said. "Buy the little one a present when he's better."

"Thank you." Nanna Flo gently squeezed his arm. "I will."

The paramedics wheeled Boo out of the ambulance and rushed him through the hospital doors with Dad running alongside the stretcher. The Wimples scrambled closely behind.

"We're here, Boo," Dad puffed. "We're right here."

The paramedics raced down the corridor until they reached the doors of the children's unit.

Levi turned and said, "We can only allow the parents inside."

India and Nanna stood panting, worry lining their faces.

"We'll be back soon," Dad promised, and he and Mom disappeared inside.

India craned her neck and saw Boo's pale face between the closing doors before they slowly blocked him from view.

India never thought it was possible for a perfectly normal heart to hurt, but seeing Boo's small body on that stretcher made her heart feel as if it were being trampled.

Nanna Flo gently took her hand.

They sat in their pajamas and fluffy hotel slippers opposite the doors.

And they waited.

~~~
~~~

The clock above the doors ticked in an endless rhythm, making each second feel long and drawn out.

Tick, tick, tick.

Stretchers sailed past, nurses pushed patients in wheelchairs, and anxious relatives searched for loved ones.

Tick, tick, tick.

India watched the doors, and each time they opened, she willed it to be Dad.

Tick, tick, tick.

When he finally appeared, India jumped from her chair into his arms. “How is he?”

Dad’s hair was ruffled and his eyes were red. “He’s a real champion. Stayed calm the whole time and did exactly what the doctors said.”

“When can we see him?” Nanna Flo asked.

“Soon. They’re running a few tests.” Dad’s voice was strained and small.

“Is he going to be OK?” India asked.

Dad held her tight. “Levi says he’s in good hands. I have to go.” He kissed her head and again disappeared through the doors.

India and her family had been in hospitals with Boo many times, but the moments when they had to wait for doctors—to hear their diagnosis, to hear if Boo was going to make it—were the hardest.

And this was the worst yet.

Their minds would race with what the doctors would say. What if it was bad news? What if this time was different? What if…

Nanna broke through her worried thoughts.

"He's a Wimple," she repeated sternly, "and we Wimples never give up. He's going to be just fine."

But there was something in her voice similar to Dad's—a slight flicker of uncertainty. She clenched her teeth, trying to hold back tears.

India had never seen Nanna Flo cry before, at least not since Grandpop's funeral, but there it was—a small tear falling down her cheek. India reached up and wiped it away.

India took her hand. "You're right, Nanna. He is going to be fine."

~~~

"Wimple family?"

Nanna and India got to their feet and stood again in a tight penguin huddle, preparing themselves for what might happen next.

The doctor spoke slowly, choosing his words carefully. "It was a particularly bad flare-up, and it will take him some time to fully recover, but Boo's quite a little fighter. He's going to be fine."

"He's going to be fine?" Nanna repeated, just to make sure.
~~~

"Yes." When the doctor smiled, his mustache curled up, so it seemed to be smiling too.

Then Nanna did something she wasn't supposed to do—she threw her skinny arms around the doctor and hugged him. "Thank you." Her muffled voice rose from his lab coat. "Thank you so much."

Nanna stayed like that for a few moments until she eventually pulled away. "Sorry."

Luckily the doctor didn't seem to mind. "That's OK. I'd probably do the same if it were my grandson. He'll be a little groggy from the medication and tired after being so unwell, so we're going to keep him for a few days, just to be safe."

"Can we see him?" India couldn't stand the idea that Boo was in a hospital room without all the Wimples around him.

"Absolutely, but he needs to rest."

Nanna and India were led through the doors and into the noisy hubbub of the children's ward until they came to Boo's room. They poked their heads inside, and, without meaning to, India gasped.

Boo looked pale and small. His head lolled to the side a little, as if it were too heavy to hold, and there was an oxygen tube beneath his nose.

Her heart again felt trampled, like a boot was stomping on her chest.

Mom and Dad gave India a hug, which made her want to cry.

Boo is going to be fine, she scolded herself. *He's a Wimple, and we Wimples never give up.*

India walked to his bedside, stepping as quietly as possible, and heard his raspy breathing.

She tried to stop it, but a single tear dripped onto Boo's hand. She quickly dabbed it away with her sleeve. She didn't allow herself to cry when Boo was sick. She never wanted him to know that she was worried or that she thought he may never come back.

She reached out and took his hand.

She wanted Boo to know that she was there, and she wasn't going anywhere.

24

CASTIGATION

(noun):

Chastisement, scolding, seriously criticized.

Everyone was shocked to hear such a stern castigation.

INDIA STOOD BESIDE BOO'S BED, holding his hand, waiting for the smallest sign that he was going to wake up, when Dad tiptoed to her side.

"You've been standing for hours," he said softly. "You should get some rest."

India shook her head. "I have to be here when Boo wakes up."

Nanna Flo was snoring in a chair, and Mom was asleep with her head on Nanna's shoulder.

Dad kept his voice low. "But you must be tired."

"He has to know I'm *here*," she snapped. But then knew she shouldn't have. It wasn't Dad's fault—none of this was. She was angry that her little brother was sick.

And she was scared.

They watched as Boo's chest rose and fell and listened to the whirring of the machine helping him breathe.

Dad wrapped his arms around India and kissed her on the head. "I'm sorry life has been so hard the last few years and that things haven't worked out quite like we expected, but you have to know how much I love being dad to you and Boo." India looked up and saw Dad's eyes shiny with tears. "I look at you both every day and wonder what I did to deserve you."

India tried to speak, but it was like the words got tangled in her throat.

"We make a good team, us Wimples, don't you think?"

India nodded, feeling even worse that she'd snapped at Dad, when Boo's eyes began to open.

"Boo?" She moved closer.

His eyes flickered. "You look terrible." His voice was scratchy.

India laughed. Her hair was a straggly mess and her pajamas were twisted and crumpled. "How kind of you to notice."

Dad stroked his cheek. "Hey, little man."

Mom woke at the sound of Dad's voice and shook Nanna's shoulder. "He's awake." They flew over to the bed and Mom gently gave Boo a teary kiss.

"You're back," she said.

Nanna's curlers flopped around her head. "Boy, did we miss you."

Boo was confused. "Did I have another flare-up?" he croaked.

"You sure did," Dad said, "and it was a doozy, but you're fine now."

Boo tried to think back, but it was all a blur. "What happened?"

"We were at the hotel," India said.

"And you were about to get into the shower," Mom added.

"I was getting ready for the bee," Boo remembered. Then he realized something else and turned to India. "Is the competition over? *Did you win?*"

"It hasn't started," India said. "But don't worry. I'm not going."

"*What?*" He dug his hands into the bed and tried to sit up, but his arms weren't strong enough. "You have to go," he wheezed.

India shook her head. "I'm staying here with you."

"Unless you became a doctor since I last saw you, there's nothing you can do."

"The competition doesn't matter."

"It *does* matter." He was tired and his breathing was heavy. "You made it to the grand final."

"But I—"

"India Wimple." Boo's voice was still weak, but India could tell he was cranky. "You listen to me. You've spent your whole life looking after me."

"Yes, but—" India started to object when Boo held up a finger.

"I haven't finished."

India closed her mouth and listened. In all the years her brother had been sick, in all the rushing to the hospital and all the tubes and doctors and late-night flare-ups, she'd never once seen him annoyed, even a little bit.

"I know you don't leave your door open at night because you worry about escaping if there's a fire." He paused to catch his breath. "I know you don't say no to sleepovers because you'd miss Mom and Dad, and I know you sneak into my room at night to check that I'm still breathing."

"You do?" Mom asked.

"Not every night," India mumbled.

Boo coughed and wheezed but wasn't about to stop.

"And then there are the times when you wake up on the floor beside me instead of in your own warm bed."

"Yes, but I don't mind."

"India." He fixed her with a stern look. "How many times have you sat by a hospital bed waiting for me to wake up? You are *not* going to sit beside *this* bed and miss the one chance in your life to let everyone know that I have the best, cleverest sister in the whole world."

Boo had never, ever been stubborn about anything in his whole life, but suddenly he was very, very good at it. "So go to the opera house now and spell like you've never spelled before."

India sighed. "Are you sure?"

"I'm more than sure," he breathed. "I'm kicking you out."

She looked at the clock on the wall. "But it starts in twenty minutes. I'll never get there in time."

"We might." Dad rubbed his chin, as if he were concocting a plan. "We just need to get there fast."

"How's our patient?" It was Levi from the ambulance.

"I'm good," Boo said, still very wheezy, "but now my sister has an emergency."

"Asthma?" Levi asked, ready to leap into action.

"No." Mom shook her head. "A spelling emergency."

Levi was confused.

"Do you know the Stupendously Spectacular Spelling Bee?" Nanna Flo asked.

"I loved that show!" Levi's eyes widened. "I used to dream about being the champion."

"Well, you could be looking at the next champion right now," Dad said, "because India has made it to the grand final."

"Really? Congratulations!"

"Yes," Mom said, "but it starts in twenty minutes."

Boo tried to look his cutest. "And we don't know how she's going to get there in time."

The Wimples were always at their best when they worked as a team, and this was some of their finest work yet.

Levi looked at his watch. "It's my dinner break—I can get you there!" He lowered his voice. "Just don't tell anyone. Who's in?"

"I'll come!" Dad cried.

Levi rattled his keys. "Let's go!"

"Thanks, Boo." India smiled.

"You're welcome. Good-luck hug?"

"Yes, please."

"You'll be great, sis," he whispered. "I know it."

Dad quickly kissed Boo, Mom, and Nanna Flo. He grabbed India's hand and called over his shoulder, "Tell the opera house we're on our way. Then turn on the TV—you're about to see a new champion!"

25

EMERGENCY

(adjective):

Crisis, dilemma, a really urgent situation.

The situation was an emergency of epic proportions.

THE RED LIGHTS OF THE ambulance blazed as it sped through the city streets, swerving in and out of traffic.

India and Dad were in the back, holding on tightly.

"Do you think we'll make it?" India asked.

Dad looked a little pale. "Of course we will, sweetheart. These guys are experts in getting places fast. In fact..." He became a shade paler as the ambulance lurched around another corner. "I think I might lie down."

He sank onto the stretcher and gripped his stomach while the siren continued to blare above them. Levi blasted the horn and cars quickly pulled out of the way. He let out a loud "*Yee-haw!*" when he spotted the Sydney Opera House. "Thar she blows!"

The ambulance sped toward the white sails and swooped into the undercover entrance before slamming on the brakes and skidding to a halt. Levi opened the doors, and he and India helped Dad onto solid ground.

"Oh, that feels better." Dad doubled over and rested his hands on his knees, not completely sure he wasn't going to be horribly sick.

"Thank you," India said to Levi.

"My pleasure. I'll be cheering for you, India."

"Coming, Dad?"

"You go inside. I'll be there as soon as I find my stomach."

India kissed him on the cheek. "I love you."

Dad wore a small smile. "And that makes me feel better already. Now go!"

"India!" It was Arlo. "You made it! Now, let's get you to that grand final." Arlo led the way once again through the long, crowded corridors. "Stand aside! Security coming through!"

When they reached the dressing room, Arlo held up two fists. "Go get 'em, India Wimple."

Trudy had been waiting for India, but her relieved smile instantly fell when she saw what India was wearing. "We'll need to do something about those clothes." It was only then that India remembered she was still in her pajamas.

"I've got just the thing."

Trudy rifled through a clothes rack and selected a dress. India quickly changed and turned to the mirror. It was a pink silk dress that rippled just above her knee and made India feel as if she were staring at somebody else.

After brushing her hair and applying a quick dab of face powder, Trudy leaned over India's shoulder and whispered, "It's time to show those other kids how it's done."

Trudy led India down a hallway to the wings of the Concert Hall stage. The air was alive with excitement. The crew was doing final lighting and camera checks, and the contestants were chatting nervously or cramming in a last-minute practice.

India had lined up behind the other contestants, catching her breath, when Rajish spotted her.

"You're here!" he said. "I looked everywhere but couldn't find you."

"Boo's in the hospital."

"Why? Is he OK?"

"He had an asthma attack." This was the first time India had said it out loud, and it made her want to cry. "It was bad, but he's going to be fine."

"I'm glad." His face lifted into a wide Rajish smile.

India smiled too. She felt instantly better.

Her hand automatically reached for her pocket, just as it did before every round, until she realized something terrible. "Oh no!"

"What is it?" Rajish asked.

"I don't have my lucky hanky."

"You have a lucky hanky?"

"Nanna Flo gave it to me. It was her dad's—my great-grandfather's. I left it at the hotel."

"Two minutes, everyone," the floor manager called.

"India Wimple," Rajish said, "you don't need a hanky to help you win."

"But Nanna Flo said it kept her dad safe during the war."

"Maybe that's true, but no lucky hanky can change the fact that you're an amazing speller."

India felt that familiar fluttering in her stomach, but not the kind that made her want to run or be sick. This one was different. This one felt...nice.

"Thank you, Rajish."

He held a spindly finger in the air. "I am only speaking the truth."

India giggled.

This time Rajish blushed. "You look very pretty."

"It's the dress."

"No, I think you always look very pretty."

"You do?"

"Of course. Good luck."

The children were led onto the stage, which is when India saw it: the Stupendously Spectacular Spelling Bee trophy. It sparkled under the stage lights and was so much bigger than she'd thought it would be.

They took their seats, and India found herself beside Summer.

Not the usual, confident Summer, but a more hunched-over, uncertain Summer, who didn't look at all excited to be there.

"Are you nervous?" India asked.

"Me?" The old Summer returned, looking the very definition of *confident*. "Why would I be *nervous*? I am the only person in this competition who has spelled every word correctly."

India was disappointed. Summer was still cranky, which must have meant her parents never made it. Her ingenious plan hadn't worked.

"It's true, but good luck anyway."

Summer eyed her warily. "Thanks."

"You're welcome."

In the audience, a man wearing a security jacket buttoned over sunflower pajamas was being shown to his seat in the front row—it was Dad, in what looked like Arlo's jacket. He sat beside the Kapoors.

All three waved and gave a thumbs-up just before the lights dimmed.

"Ten seconds, everyone." The floor manager held her hand in front of the camera lens and counted down. "We're on in five… four…three…two…"

The theme music began and the audience burst into applause.

Philomena Spright drifted onto the stage like a ballroom dancer. "Welcome to the grand final of the Stupendously Spectacular Spelling Bee, coming to you live from one of the world's most *stupendously spectacular* venues, the Sydney Opera House." She was her resplendent best in an elegant white gown with her signature ice-cream-swirl hair. "We have the best and brightest spellers before us tonight, but our job today is to find the ultimate winner, so let's begin."

Philomena explained the rules before calling the first speller to the microphone.

While India waited for her turn, she practiced spelling each word, seeing them clearly in her head. There was no jumble of letters, no rewriting of words again and again on her hand. For the first time, being part of the spelling bee felt no more frightening than lying on her living room floor in Yungabilla on a Friday night.

Transcendent.

Delectable.

Phenomenal.

The audience sat as still as glass, waiting nervously for Philomena to pronounce the answer right or wrong.

Rajish and India swapped smiles each time they spelled a word correctly.

As the rounds progressed and the words became harder, more contestants misspelled their words and had to leave the stage.

An hour went by, chairs emptied and dreams of being the champion faded, until there were only three spellers left: Rajish, Summer, and India.

Each time they approached the microphone, they were presented with a more difficult challenge.

Metamorphosis.

Transmogrification.

Chrysalis.

They'd been spelling for over two hours.

Rajish was next.

Philomena held another card before her. "*Scheherazadian.*"

Rajish paused before asking, "Could I have the definition please?"

"This is an adjective deriving from Scheherazade, the imaginative queen who narrated stories in *The Arabian Nights.*"

Rajish closed his eyes and his lips moved silently. He was taking longer than usual to answer. India knew he could do it, but she crossed her fingers for him extra tight just in case.

Finally, he began. "Scheherazadian. S-c-h-e-h-e-r..." He paused and closed his eyes again, as if he were looking at the word one more time to make sure. "a-z-a-d-i-e-n."

The audience waited. There was absolute quiet.

Philomena paused for effect. India already knew what she was going to say. She saw Mr. Kapoor's lower lip tremble.

"That is...incorrect, I'm afraid. The spelling is s-c-h-e-h-e-r-a-z-a-d-i-a-n, which means, sadly, we have to say goodbye." She turned to the audience. "Please join me in congratulating Rajish on being one of our top three spellers in the country."

The audience clapped. Rajish's dad wiped away a tear and cried out above them all, "Bravo, my son!"

Rajish winked at India as he walked off stage. It was a wink that said, *You can do it.*

"And now for the moment of truth." Philomena invited Summer and India to stand beside the microphone. "Good luck to you both."

India tried to catch Summer's eye for a last good-luck glance, but Summer kept her gaze firmly ahead.

The parade of words continued.

Reminiscences.

Frabjous.

Peripeteia.

Each one was spelled perfectly.

Summer stepped up to the microphone, eager for the next.

"*Consanguineous,*" Philomena said. "This is an adjective meaning of the same blood or descended from the same ancestor, like your biological parents."

India saw Summer flinch, just a little, but she straightened instantly.

"Con-sanguineous." Summer actually stammered a little as she said it.

She looked down at her shoes. They sparkled under the studio lights. But she said nothing.

"Thirty seconds," Philomena repeated, jolting Summer to life.

She began to spell. "C-o-n..."

But something caught her eye—or someone. Summer squinted into the audience.

It was her mom and dad. They'd made it. They were really here!

A bell sounded through the hall.

"I'm sorry, Summer," Philomena said. "Time is up, which means you forfeit your turn."

There was a brief moment when Summer didn't move, until she nodded and, to India's surprise, smiled.

Philomena invited India to the microphone, the card for the next word held firmly in her hands.

"India Wimple, if you spell this next word correctly, you will be our new champion. Are you ready?"

After months of practicing, and all those nerves and the

nagging voice inside her head, India Wimple had made it to the grand final. Just thinking about it made her teeter for an instant, but she grabbed the mic stand and steadied herself just in time. "I think I am."

From the front row, Dad sat in his pajamas and security jacket with a grin plastered across his face. He gave his usual Dad wave.

India was indeed ready.

"Your word is *transcendent*."

India glanced at Summer, who didn't seem bothered at all that she hadn't spelled her last word. She even seemed...happy.

"This is an adjective meaning to go beyond ordinary limits, to surpass or exceed."

All around the country, people watched India Wimple stand onstage at the Sydney Opera House—from Saint Michael's Hospital to the prime minister's residence, from the lobby of the Hotel Grand to the packed community hall in a small town called Yungabilla.

"If I used it in a sentence, I could say, *Her achievements could only be described as transcendent.*"

"Transcendent," India began. "T-r-a-n-s-c-e-n-d-e-n-t. Transcendent."

Rajish's smile lit up from the side of the stage.

Philomena, who never liked to reveal the answer too soon, slowly and carefully began to speak. "India Wimple…that is correct! You are…our new Stupendously Spectacular Spelling Bee champion!"

"I am?"

The audience laughed.

"You most certainly are."

India was caught in the sudden dazzle of flashing lights and confetti falling from the ceiling. A rush of applause and cheers filled the hall.

Dad was escorted onto the stage, where he threw his arms around his little girl and swung her into the air.

Philomena lifted the trophy from its stand. "It is my pleasure to present you with the official spelling bee trophy."

India reached out and took the handle, but it was heavier than she'd expected, and she almost dropped it. Dad caught it just in time and helped her hold it in the air while cameras flashed and clicked.

When everyone quieted down, Philomena Spright continued. "As always, here is your five-hundred-dollar gift card for Mr. Trinket's Book Emporium."

India clutched the envelope. She had seen the gift card handed out to so many children in the past, and she instantly ran through her head all the books she would buy. "Thank you."

"You certainly earned it, but we have something else."

Dad took the trophy and India tried to slow her breathing, but it wasn't working.

"Here is a check for five thousand dollars." The audience gasped, and India held the piece of paper carefully. She was absolutely certain this was the most exciting moment of her life, but Philomena wasn't finished yet. "Money you are going to need, because you and your family are off on a glorious vacation to the destination of your choice!"

Now it was Dad's turn to nearly drop the trophy and for India to save it from crashing to the ground. The audience laughed in relief.

Including Philomena. "With the whole world at your fingertips, where would you like to go?"

India Wimple instantly knew the answer. "There's a small beach in India where my mom and dad met." India looked at Dad, whose eyes brimmed with tears. "I think it's time the Wimple family went there."

This, of course, made Dad blubber even more.

The audience offered one collective sigh, and even Philomena wiped away a tear. "Is there anything else you'd like to say?"

India took a deep breath. "I'm here today because of my family: Mom, Dad, Nanna Flo, and my brother, Boo—and also the town of Yungabilla. I've always loved spelling, but I'd never have been brave enough to enter this competition if it hadn't been for them." She looked directly into the camera. "This is for you, Boo, the best brother in the whole world.

"But I also want to thank Summer and Rajish." Summer looked up. "Two of the best spellers I know." The floor manager ushered them both to the center of the stage. "I think they're champions too."

There was another burst of applause and camera flashes as all three stood together. This gave Rajish's dad another chance to stand up and cheer, "Bravo!"

Philomena turned to the camera. "That's it for another Stupendously Spectacular Spelling Bee. Thank you to our *superlative* spellers and to you, our *magnanimous* audience. Would you like the chance to stand on this very stage, just like India Wimple? If you think you have what it takes, why not sign up? Because the next spelling bee champion could be *you*!"

As the theme music played, Rajish's parents hurried onto the stage, and there was an explosion of kisses and hugs.

India noticed something else through all the commotion. Two more people were hurrying across the stage.

"Summer, darling!" The woman wore a figure-hugging dress and a long, fine coat, while the man followed in a finely tailored suit and silk cravat.

Summer threw herself into their arms. "Mom! Dad! You made it!"

"We couldn't stay away," her dad said. "Not after we received that message from your friend."

"My *friend*?"

"Yes, your friend India."

Summer shot a confused glance at India, who simply shrugged.

"When we spoke yesterday, we thought you preferred us not to be here. We were thrilled when India told us that wasn't true. So we canceled everything and asked Nathaniel to fly us here immediately."

"You did?"

"Why, yes! We didn't want to miss your big moment."

India couldn't help but notice that Summer didn't look like the pushy, mouthy girl they first saw in the Hotel Grand. She looked like someone altogether nicer.

"And to celebrate, we've booked a table at La Rendezvous, your favorite restaurant," her dad said. "And we warned them we'd be bringing our very own champion." He held out his hand. "Care to join us?"

Her mom held hers out too, and Summer gripped them both. "I would love to."

As she left the stage holding her parents' hands, Summer smiled at India and mouthed the words *thank you*.

And India silently replied, *You're welcome.*

26

SPLENDIFEROUS

(adjective):

Excellent, wonderful, superbly marvelous.

Who would have thought such a bumpy start would lead to such a splendiferous end?

THERE'S REALLY NOT MUCH MORE to say about the Wimples and the Stupendously Spectacular Spelling Bee.

India Wimple appeared in newspapers and on TV shows all over the country and didn't mind the attention at all—she even enjoyed it—but what was really special was the barbecue held in her honor at the Yungabilla Club. Everyone in town showed up, the school band played tunes that seemed somehow familiar, and the mayor gave a speech. For dessert, Mrs. O'Donnell baked a giant-size blueberry cheesecake with a message written on top that said:

WELCOME HOME, INDIA

WE KNEW YOU COULD DO IT

India Wimple still adored her family, and that was still the most important thing about her, but she was no longer terribly, horribly shy. She was ingenious and fearless and a champion speller.

And she'd made a new friend.

Over one million people watched India become the new Stupendously Spectacular Spelling Bee champion, including one very special person, who sent a very special messenger to the Wimple home, who they discovered when they answered a knock at the door.

India stood before a tall, well-groomed man who she instantly recognized.

"Mr. Noble? What are you doing here?"

It was indeed Mr. Noble, and when he opened his mouth to answer, Dad appeared beside India. "Mr. Noble? What a pleasant surprise."

"Why thank you, I—"

Nanna Flo squeezed between Dad and India. "Who is it?"

"Mr. Noble," Dad said.

"Why has he come to see us?"

"We're not sure," India answered. "He hasn't told us yet."

"I have come to—" Mr. Noble tried again, but Boo wiggled between them all.

"Mr. Noble. What are you doing in Yungabilla?"

"I am here to—"

"Ah, Mr. Noble." Mom this time. "What can we do for you?"

Mr. Noble sighed, wondering if anyone else was going to pop their head out of the house. "On behalf of the prime minister, the official patron of the spelling bee, I would like to present India with a special gift in honor of being the new champion."

Mr. Noble handed over a rather heavy package and a card. India opened the card and read it out loud:

Dear India,

It gave me enormous pleasure to watch you become the Stupendously Spectacular Spelling Bee champion. My family and I watched it last Friday in our pajamas. The terriers were very excited—I'm sure they recognized you. I can only imagine how thrilled you must have been—and how much your family is embarrassing you even more now by telling everyone how wonderful they think you are. As a token of my esteem and admiration, I would like to offer you a small gift. It is the very one I fell asleep on so many times as a boy. It was given to me by my father, who always believed in me.

With best wishes,

Your friend and fellow logophile,

The Prime Minister

"Logophile?" Dad asked.

"Word lover," Boo explained.

India tore off the wrapping paper. Inside was a battered, well-worn dictionary.

India thought it was one of the nicest presents she'd ever been given.

~~~

So we leave this story for the last time on a beach, in the sunshine, with the Wimples reclining on deck chairs.

Nanna Flo, Dad, Mom, Boo, and India. And beside them were the Kapoors.

India and Rajish sat beside Mom and Dad, who told stories about the first time they met. Mr. and Mrs. Kapoor held hands and laughed, just like they used to before the spelling bee.

Boo had a book nestled on his lap and was reading fascinating facts about India out loud. "Did you know shampoo, chess, and Chutes and Ladders were invented in India?"
~~~

“No,” India said, sipping her drink, “but I do know they have the world’s most delicious mango lassis.”

Nanna Flo opened her bag, wondering which of the treats she’d taken from the breakfast bar she should eat first. “Banana, anyone?”

She handed out her stash of fruit while Rajish took a sip of his coconut juice. “It has been very nice getting to know you, India Wimple.”

“You too, Rajish Kapoor.”

“But there’s something I’ve been meaning to tell you,” he said, suddenly very serious. “And you may not like it.”

"What is it?"

"I think you're wrong."

"About what?"

"I think you *are* good at this people thing." His smile lifted his cheeks. "In fact, I think you may be better than anyone I know. You just didn't realize it."

"Thank you, Rajish."

He held his finger in the air and whispered so his father wouldn't hear. "I am only speaking the truth."

India laughed, and, just like that, a terribly, horribly shy girl from Yungabilla, who became the Stupendously Spectacular Spelling Bee champion, dug her toes into the warm sand and settled back onto her deck chair on a beach in India, where the story of the Wimples first began.

About the Author

Deborah Abela is short and not very brave, which may explain why she writes books about spies, ghosts, soccer legends, and children living in a flooded city battling sea monsters and sneaker waves. When she was in fourth grade, Deb had a wonderful teacher called Miss Gray, who made reading and spelling spectacular fun. Deb has won awards for her books but mostly hopes to be as brave as her characters.

Find out more about what she's been up to at deborahabela.com.